The Darling
of Kandahar

Pentru Grabriela.
cu drag

(signature)

17 iunie 2015

Cover design by Debbie Geltner
Cover image by Debbie Geltner, Mirela Ivanciu
Photo of Author by Martine Doyon
Printed and bound in Canada by Marquis Book Printing Inc.

Library and Archives Canada Cataloguing in Publication

Mihali, Felicia, 1967-
    The darling of Kandahar / Felicia Mihali.

Also issued in electronic format.
ISBN 978-0-9878317-0-5

    I. Title.

PS8576.I295343D37 2012   C813'.6   C2011907679-9

LITERARY FICTION
Linda Leith Publishing Inc.
www.lindaleith.com/publishing

.ll.

The Darling
of Kandahar

a novel

FELICIA MIHALI

LINDA LEITH
PUBLISHING

A life spent in the company of foreigners inevitably involves misunderstandings and mistakes.
Linda Leith
Marrying Hungary

Live in any place long enough and you learn to call it home.
Noah Richler
This is my Country, What is Yours?

You've all heard beautiful stories told by an old woman sitting in a chair in front of a window. You listen to her as she remembers the good old days and tells you about her great loves.

I am going to tell you my story, too, though I am not old at all. Young women have stories to tell, too, and may even have experienced great love. Outside, big snowflakes will be falling, because you are in Canada. My desk is set right in front of the window where, at this time of day, the light is reduced by the shadow cast by a big building across St. Lawrence Boulevard, The Main.

My name is Irina, I am 24 years old, and my parents moved to Montreal when I was four. My name is that of an old Byzantine empress, but I was born in Transylvania. For those unfamiliar with horror movies, I should add this is Dracula's country. My mother, who is Romanian, gets angry every time someone associates her with the character imagined by the Irish writer Bram Stoker. The myth originates with Vlad the Impaler who, when he was locked up in Bran Castle by his Hungarian enemies, became known for killing rats to alleviate his boredom.

A few years after their arrival here, and shortly before their divorce, my parents took me on a visit to Romania. In Canada, they had come to think that coming from the same place as Dracula was nothing to be ashamed of, for the vampire was no more than a tourist attraction. So they decided to go back to see those places again with new eyes.

The castle where the Romanian sovereign was imprisoned is one of the most beautiful in the country. An old fortress set on high cliffs and protected all around by mountains, this was one of the best lookout points during the Middle Ages. Paths leading to its wooden door were concealed by a thick forest of conifers in those days, and its keep, parapets and watchtowers look even today as though they are straight out of a fairy tale. The stone walls are about a metre thick, so that the chambers stay cool and shady even in hot weather. What still comes to my mind is a small garden with a bottomless spring in the middle, the story of which I no longer remember.

At the time Bran Castle was built, the Romanian territory was divided into three small provinces: Hungarian Transylvania, Wallachia, and Moldavia, which enjoyed some autonomy though threatened by the Russians to the north. As this is the historical part of my story, I have to tell you that my father's reason for leaving Romania was the fact that Russia was always a deceitful ally, even after the fall of the Communists. In the Middle Ages, fortresses like Bran Castle were necessary, he said, because people in Transylvania had to defend their territory against their Romanian brothers from the south rather than against the Turks, who were our declared enemies.

My mother knew my father's opinions, and she used to just let him talk. Once we set foot in Canada, though, she couldn't stand hearing about the old conflicts between Romanians and Hungarians. But those stories are not the reason my parents separated.

During that trip back to Romania, my parents studied every nook and cranny, every stone, and every path. They tried to understand how these places could have awakened the imagination of that Irishman who, rather than going back to the ghosts of his own history, preferred instead to delve into the tragic past of the Romanians, as though it weren't enough that they had already had a thousand years of being the victims of false interpretations. Because of him, here we are carrying a bloodsucker on our shoulders for ever.

My parents had always thought the Dracula story was nonsense. Now, with their new Canadian identity, they saw it differently. They paid attention to the story for the first time just so as to come up with counter-arguments. The day before they separated, there was only one point they still agreed on, and that was that Vlad the Impaler ended up not as a vampire, but in the hands of the Turks.

I guess it's time I told you about my family.

My parents came from a province where the two solitudes lived side by side on much the same principle as here. My father belonged to the smaller, richer Hungarian solitude, and my mother to the bigger, but poorer, Romanian one. As in Quebec, the Romanian solitude had survived because of its language, its religion and its population numbers, which might be the requirements for the survival of any cultural group.

My father, an old-stock Hungarian, rather despised the Romanians, especially after his marriage ended. He was too proud to accept that his mother could have been right when she warned him about Romanians, but he did trust his experience in Canada, which taught him that people cannot wipe out their racial – or what Canadians call cultural – differences, and that group memories arise when you least expect them.

The disconnect produced by multicultural policies has clearly had some effect here. Have you ever asked yourself why the word culture, which once referred to all that the human mind has produced, has now come to include the colour of your skin? In order not to be offended by this, ethnic minorities see themselves honored by the term cultural, which Canadian politicians use in attempts to diminish the impact of a dark face or a spicy meal.

In Transylvania, people were not too worried about the metaphysics of human differences. All they knew for certain was that every Romanian family considered a Hungarian lad was a good choice for their daughter.

Once they landed in Montreal, my parents based themselves in this no-man's-land separating the Francophone and Anglophone sides of the city. Immigrants were supposed to fill the space between the two communities, but what they really did was increase the gap between them. Their task was not in fact to reconcile the two groups, but to make them more foreign in each other's eyes. Each time newcomers go to one side, the other reopens the old controversy.

My mother now belonged to the French solitude, bigger but less wealthy, while my father, who worked for an English company, was on the other side. Each half-heartedly defended the values of the group to which they belonged. And neither made much of an effort to score points against the other. They were doing their best to make a peaceful life for themselves in their new country.

It was too late for them to get into national debates. My mother learned that from my father before they separated. What they lacked was anger. They were too old, and they had the sense that this was a conflict that did not concern them. Let them solve their own problems! Two solitudes is it? What happens, then, to the third one, the lonely immigrant side, left on its own or, even worse, caught up in a political game and sacrificed in multicultural speeches?'

So my parents learned how easy it is to steer clear of the kinds of conflicts that can make people capable of bloodshed. How much better it is not to be torn apart by historical quarrels between Arabs and Jews, Chinese and Japanese, Indians and Sikhs, Pashtuns and Tadjiks, Uzbeks and Hazaras. Only once did my father propose an idea my mother disagreed with. "They don't hate each other any more," he said. "That's because they have someone else to hate. We are their common enemy."

My mother decided to keep her new partner away from all these national arguments inherited from her marriage to my father. Have you any idea what it's like to be associated with Dracula? To be taken for somebody other than the person you really are? You feel a certain pride in things that do not make you proud, and you represent things that have nothing to do with you. And there's more to it than this, for immigrants always bring their problems with them when they move to a new country. It's a Canadian writer who said this.

I myself brought nothing, because I was too young when I came here. I don't even remember what language I spoke. Maybe it was more Hungarian than Romanian, but after our arrival my mother didn't want me to use the local variation of my father's language except this single expression: solnitza, paprika, horinka. These are the three things supposedly most cherished by Hungarians: salt, paprika and booze. It was her little revenge, because my father did not have any scornful phrases in Romanian that he could torment my mother with. If you want to hurt someone, you have to speak his language. My father eventually figured that out.

Sometimes, people ask me where I come from, and when

I say Canada they know the Canada I am talking about. This is because my name contains too many z's, c's, and t's, even though I'm listed under the letter H in the telephone directory.

I still live with my mother, who remarried to a sailor who lives at home one month in four. He is a Quebecer. As with any Quebecer who becomes part of an immigrant family, he has to keep quiet about his separatist feelings. With mixed couples, the old-stock, died-in-the-wool Quebecer learns, bit by bit, to laugh at the newcomers' jokes about them and to accept the way they use Quebec swearwords. They even become a little jealous of the way a Chinese, an Arab or a Polish immigrant pronounces tabarouette and ostie.

According to my mother, her husband is a good guy with no big flaws. Did I say his name is Pierre? Luckily, though, his parents didn't call him Pierre-something, and his family name only has one part to it. Otherwise imagine my mother's embarrassment; she has always had trouble with foreign names, even that of my own father.

When Pierre comes ashore, he spends his time visiting second-hand goods dealers and garage sales. The shelves in our apartment go right up to the ceiling in every room, and they are crowded with knick-knacks and are as dusty as an antique shop. Pierre picks up all kinds of stuff – ornamental pumpkins, painted eggs, tiny porcelain statues, odd cups, bronze candlesticks, native crafts. He doesn't buy any of it for himself. It's all for my mother, who is a painter.

My mother has never worked in Canada. Since coming here, she has been a student, taking short breaks in between different university courses. She has a B.A and an M.A. in History and another B.A. and M.A. in Art History, but don't ask her why she studied these subjects. The question drives her crazy. Why should a woman, or a man, have a specific reason for studying? Is passion or interest not enough? All my mother wants is to be educated, stay at home, and dedicate herself to her work. Isn't that wonderful? When you think that women in other parts of the world are forced by their men to stay at home and are unhappy about it.

She started painting under the guidance of some artists from the Romanian community when she was doing her B.A. in Art History. The community has lots of artists who made a name for themselves long ago; here, they have to do menial work to make ends meet.

More or less self-educated as an artist, my mother slowly started showing her work in small cafés downtown, but no one paid much attention. Did she even want that? It doesn't seem so. When a supposed literary agent in the community offered to take on my mother's career, she hung up on the younger woman, accusing her of being a spy.

My mother wants nothing to do with pressures from the outside world, or with any responsibility either to produce or earn money. She hates everything that gets in the way of her routine, anything that could affect the time she drinks her coffee and waters the basil and rosemary plants on her balcony. She doesn't do much the rest of the day, either. She has few friends left, and she doesn't go out except to shop. All she does is paint.

Not that she produces very much. A small canvas sometimes takes her months, for she has a baroque taste for details she is forever adding and removing. Lately, she has been drawing knights and Muses, and she's especially fond of Mnemosyne, muse of memory. She also likes Clio, muse of History, and Calliope, because my mother also writes poetry. Her canvases are piling up in our two storerooms: she doesn't sell her work, nor does she give any of it away as presents.

She doesn't hate winter or get depressed by it. Winter

forces her to stay on the sofa all day long and not move except to the kitchen and the bathroom. When I'm out, she has the apartment to herself. She enjoys this realm that belongs to her, where she feels really free. My mother has built her happiness on loneliness and on a mysterious empire of thoughts. What does she think about all day long?

Can you see how annoying it is, talking about yourself? Which in fact means talking about everybody around you: family, classmates, lovers. As individuals, we're not much more than a bunch of connections with others. Which is comforting enough, since it guarantees a kind of posterity even after our physical disappearance.

I have to go back to the knick-knacks.

When my mother first knew Pierre, she used to take him to garage sales. To Pierre, the idea of looking for treasures hidden in the streets of Montreal was new. Garage sales in Quebec seemed to him to be nothing more than a good opportunity for middle-class families to throw junk away. It was better to clear a house of old paintings, frames, mirrors, sticks of furniture, dried flowers, puppets, plastic toys, and paper-flower books and sell it all than dump it on the street and wait for the garbage man.

Because they move house frequently, Quebecers are not used to saving or amassing fortunes for future generations. Houses built of wood and paperboard could burn down at any time, so what was the point of keeping souvenirs? This country has no great attachment to physical mementos; when a place is emptied, they just pull down the building. In Quebec, memory has to be active, something that's always in motion. Why else would they hang *Je me souviens* on the back of their cars?

This country doesn't want to fall in love with things. It doesn't want to take care of things or fix them, and it especially doesn't want to feel regret. Clothes, shoes, furniture, cars – nothing is kept, except the French language. They teach their children not to owe anything to anyone: young people are taught to build everything with their own hands. No one wants anything from anyone if a legacy means dealing with troublesome clauses, mysterious deals, and shady notaries. They're afraid to show gratitude to anyone. When you owe gratitude, you are less free. Ancestors and the past are dangerous, for they make you look back, and people here are always looking ahead. Memories are just B-movie plots.

In Orhan Pamuk's *My Name is Red*, a master miniaturist shows the man who comes to kill him a 300-year-old Mongol inkwell. Up to a certain period in our history, people valued an object for its age and for the place it came from; the more distant, the better. Nowadays, when something is Chinese it means it's cheap and of poor quality. For my mother, however, "Made in China" still grants objects of any caliber and purpose the nobility of the mysterious unknown.

Pierre also became the prisoner of this philosophy. Through the eyes of my immigrant mother, he was discovering another side to his own country. Strangers have this peculiar capacity to change things. They have an ancient practice of granting new life to any old junk. At the beginning of their relationship, my mother wanted old objects to put in her still-life paintings, and Pierre was as amazed as a child by the new uses my mother made of things they had found on the street. When she changed her approach, focusing instead on Greek mythology and the Muses, she stopped going to garage sales. Not Pierre. Bargain hunting overlapped in some way with his vocation as a traveler.

When he was not at sea, he sailed through the neighbourhoods of Montreal searching for hidden treasures. He had soon accumulated a lot of stuff, which did not upset my mother. The advantage remarried women have is that they get cleverer: they finally understand that it's enough to act in silence without going all out to convince your partner to change his mind. When Pierre was away, she simply threw things away, starting with what he had bought a while back. She had noticed he wasn't interested in what was in the house. He just bought stuff, presented it to my mother proudly, and then forgot about it. This is why there is still room for new things on our shelves.

Is this about Pierre or about my mother?

Pierre does not like beer but brandy, because on board the ship the sailors drink spirits, which are stronger and take up less room. I won't comment on Pierre's surprise at some Eastern European curiosities. My mother is not eager to let him know too much about her old identity or to cook him authentic Romanian meals such as a soup made from cow's stomach or a dish of beans with neck of pork. I believe, though, that it is not just her exotic appeal that persuaded Pierre to choose her out of all his neighbours – because, yes, they used to live next door to each other. What attracted them to each other is none of our business.

I don't know when I am going to start talking about myself. I am already involved in all of this though, and especially in my mother's apartment.

I did not grow up in this building. After my mother got divorced, she moved into a cheap one-bedroom place, and we lived there for a while. At night, my mother slept on the sofa in the dining room, and I had my own room. When she met Pierre, they moved into a two-bedroom, and I moved out to live with my boyfriend, Manuel. When he and I broke up, my mother invited me to come back and live with her and continue my studies, as she was alone almost eight months of the year.

Pierre was not against this; I suppose he hoped to keep an eye on my mother's possible lovers. He let me choose my room, the bigger one, which I then gave to my mother because she often worked in her bedroom. We arranged the apartment to our taste, concentrating on the dining room and balcony. Pierre was just a visitor, and he was welcomed and treated with great care, the way you treat a visitor. When he was at sea, we both breathed a sigh of relief, but what's wrong with that? You have to admit that having a man around makes women waste an awful lot of energy. In Quebec, the need for a male partner is clear, especially in winter, although there is no entrance here to clear of snow, since we live in an apartment block. Pierre and my mother are respectful to each other, and both know their place, their obligations and their rights as part of the couple.

I contribute to the rent because, unlike my mother, I both work and study. Does she think this is a good idea? Not really, but, wise as she has become, she does not try to make me change my mind. Her philosophy of life is that people should do one thing at a time: first study, then work. She would like me to become a remarkable person, or at least persevere in something; this is the dream of any immigrant mother. My mother should not judge other people too severely, though, or she might herself be judged.

It may be that I exaggerate. I think my mother accepts me as I am, with the choices I have made, just as I accept her. I study with pleasure, but as no pleasure lasts forever, I often have to take a break. My mother no longer lectures me, as in the past, telling me what to eat, how to manage my money, what to wear, all of which she then said all over again. The times I come home or go out are not under discussion any more. But don't worry. There's really no need to. I'm not at all excessive.

When I come home, the first thing I do is smoke a cigarette with my mother. Yes, she is a smoker, and I learned this from her. Everyone else condemns her, except for me; even Pierre, who is a smoker, too. My mother eventually convinced me to make a few good choices in my life, so why should she be judged only on this? I started off stealing cigarettes from her packet, and when she found out she was very sad, but she didn't dare punish me. How could she forbid me a sin that she herself practiced so assiduously?

My mother cannot give up cigarettes. Smoking is part of her loneliness, her art, her soul. Cigarettes are the good part of her life, the Aladdin's lamp, her flying carpet, the sacred smoke from Pythia's temple. Everything makes sense in my mother's routine when, after an hour, she vanishes behind her thick menthol cloud. Without it, a terrible loneliness defeats her, and she does not want that. Fragrant candles burn day and night in our apartment, as in a cathedral, to get rid of the smell of cigarettes.

If there were something else to reproach my mother for, it would be that Radou still visits her when Pierre is away. He is a Romanian painter, and it is no secret to anyone, except for Pierre, that my mother was the model for all of his nudes. She is quite chubby now, but charming, with her small shoulders and tiny ankles. She disguises her belly under a knitted shawl and her neck under heavy jewelry. Her head is often wrapped in a scarf. During the Radou years, she was skinny.

She has a painting in her bedroom of a naked woman riding an eagle, but back to front, which is to say the woman's head faces the animal's tail. The only clothing the figure is wearing is a red hat sewn with pearls. She looks straight at the spectator, her right hand on her belly. Her breasts are perfectly round, like two apples that happen to be attached to her chest. Her face is unrecognizable.

But how could you be jealous of Radou, who is now so old? Deep wrinkles crisscross his cheeks and forehead, and his thinning hair has almost turned white. One of our few visitors spoke about his passion for gambling and of his recent desire to end his days in France. This made my mother miserable. She never speaks to me about Radou, and his rare visits make her even more silent.

Another person who used to visit is a woman writer who got upset after the opening of one of my mother's shows. I remember this because I was at home when my mother explained over the phone why she did not go to the event. She said she had eaten something that had gone off and had a huge cold sore on her bottom lip. This was not true, and the woman at the end of the phone knew this.

The day of the opening, my mother stared out the window for a long time, wrapped in her plush red dressing gown, sipping her coffee, and pulling on her cigarette. It was a wretched, rainy day. How could she leave her cozy nest to face the cloudy sky and the empty streets? My mother no longer did things she didn't want to do. She did not have to. If that writer were really her friend, she would have known not to expect my mother to go out on a day like that.

Instead of wisely accepting this excuse, the writer chose not to call us anymore. My mother did not seem to suffer as a result. The void around her did not bother her. This is a disease that still affects her, and there's a name for it: agoraphobia.

Why am I going on about my mother?

Because it seems to me I myself am showing more and more noticeable symptoms of agoraphobia. The fact that I never call my friends is taken badly. Some of my friends believe that this is a way of making myself more interesting or more desirable, which is not the case. My physical appearance encourages this interpretation, and there are people who think me proud, which is not something I have ever had reason to feel guilty about.

If I had to talk about myself, I would admit that I have innocent pleasures and curiosities. I like to watch people's mouths after they have eaten a piece of cake, for example. They keep on salivating, and the words they utter look like crumbs stuck between their teeth and on their gums.

I also have to admit that my credit cards are maxed out. This bad behavior does not come from any complex or rebellion against my mother. She always tells me to pay my debts on time.

I am beautiful, which gives me a certain freedom. I don't have to make much effort to please people, because I know they like me anyway. I have big breasts and wide hips, which happens to be the title of a Chinese novel. Don't forget, I'm studying literature, so it's easy for me to come out with literary references.

The story I'm going to tell showed me I am even more beautiful than I thought. The events that have changed my life took place in the summer, which is the season when girls can take advantage of their appealing nature. In Quebec, people say that young women do not marry in winter, and it's easy to understand why.

I love the company of my friends. I like spending time in cafés, but not in bars; I've enough of bars, having worked in one. In summer, I like swimming and sleeping in the park under the shade of a tree. I like shopping for small things, like everybody else. I like listening to gossip about my friends. I eat chocolate, I drink coffee, and I like red wine. It isn't trendy to do drugs, and I don't. I am nei-

ther solemn nor gloomy nor excessively pessimistic. I don't
like double-talk, symbols, or parables: that's my mother's
domain, and I take after my father, too.

You wouldn't be wrong if you called me ordinary. As
ordinary as anybody on this earth who lives and dies for
unknown reasons. There is no merit in being born in such
and such a place, nor of dying in the most unexpected
country, and so our mistakes should not be judged too severely, should they? When you have no merit, you're not
guilty, either. It was Yannis who thought that.

Why do my classmates hate me? Because they have
trouble getting me to join them. Once I get home, it's impossible to get me to go out again. Just like my mother, I excuse myself with the most ridiculous inventions, anything
to be left alone. As soon as I put on my dressing gown and
my polar-bear slippers and sit down on the couch next to
my mother, nothing can get me to get dressed again. After
having walked on windy streets in autumn, snowy streets in
winter, boiling streets in summer, no one can persuade me
to head outside and take the métro again.

Some people get angry for no good reason. The routine that makes me happy might well drive another person
crazy or make them suicidal. All I need is a good shower
after a day of work. My mother often pushes me to accept
invitations, and the only argument she can come up with is,
What are you going to do when you grow older? I suspect
she just wants the flat to herself. But every time I refuse to
go to a party, my mother feels secure. She looks the way
she looks when she's lost something and is not sad about
it. When the phone rings, she doesn't even bother turning
down the volume on the TV. She knows I won't be long.

Talking about clothing, mine reveals my unsophisticated
nature. I dress simply, winter and summer. I have long hair
but I don't fix it in complicated styles. I usually wear it

down or in a ponytail. To get an idea of what I usually wear, just take a look at the picture in the second issue of *Maclear's* magazine. I'm wearing a pair of jeans and a black T-shirt that shows my breasts, but decently. You can make out my nipples. My classmates tell me I am very sexy, but that was just a casual outfit for a summer day.

What they do not know is that in this picture my breasts look like those in Radou's painting: two round apples just about to fall. That image is of my mother at her most glorious. My own life, too, has changed since the day that photographer from *Maclear's* asked me to pose for the cover.

In Quebec, summer is the short hunting season when men search desperately for somebody to spend the winter with. Women are a kind of provision that allows men to survive this horrible season. This may seem funny, but spending the cold season alone can be fatal in certain places. A good woman is someone who's good to winter with.

I can't resist telling you about a scene from the TV series *Pure laine*, in which an African man has married a Quebec woman. In one episode, the school principal gets into an argument with an immigrant teacher, telling him he does not understand anything about their tragedies. Do you know what it means to wait a whole winter to get a wife? she shouts. No, he doesn't know, because he's from Rwanda. A comedy, as you can see.

The story really begins at lunchtime on that summer day when I was on campus with two of my friends. A young man came up to our group, said hello, looked at each of us in turn, and then asked me if I would be willing to pose for the front cover of a national magazine for an issue ranking universities. I laughed and accepted without hesitation.

The young man told me to follow him to an alley

where another man was waiting for us, holding a plastic Le Château bag. When he saw us, he took an academic gown and a mortarboard out of the bag. They figured out where I should stand, facing the sun, wearing that stupid outfit. The photographer tried more than dozen shots before declaring he was satisfied. It didn't take long. After ten minutes, they helped me take off the gown and even helped tidy my hair, which had got messy because of the mortarboard. I still wonder about the briefness of things that can later on rouse huge emotions, when they do not destroy you. Ten minutes is long enough to kill a person. The two men thanked me warmly and then left, telling me to look out for the next issue of *Maclear's*.

When I returned to my friends, they asked me how much I was paid. I let an Ah! of surprise escape, because it had not occurred to me to ask for money. You see how much I am like my mother? Making money has never been a priority for us. Did I already have a feeling that this would be something that really mattered to me?

As for my childhood, I have to say this was a calm, even boring, period of my life. Except for my parents' divorce – which didn't come as a shock to anyone – nothing particularly sad or dramatic happened. I loved my father, because he was nice to me, stern with my mother, but fair to both of us. I had no problem with his authority, because I never disagreed with my elders – parents, teachers, or bosses. In all my life, I never once shouted at my parents. I obeyed them as I thought their requests perfectly matched my needs, and they had my complete agreement.

The lack of conflict between us made my father's departure bearable. Except for the fact that he wasn't living with us anymore, our personal relationship continued as before. I found my mother's presence and my father's money reassuring. In Quebec, many children expect no more than that.

My father never asked me to spend weekends or summer holidays with his new family. He probably knew that meeting her father's new wife is no fun for a girl. There were no regrets on either side. My mother lived alone for a few years, and if she had any boyfriends, she saw them at their place.

I always went to private schools, which was my father's decision. My mother was convinced that a child who really wants to learn does so even in the worst possible school, but my father only trusted polite surroundings. What drove my mother crazy were the fees charged for this. It wasn't a matter of money, because she is not a stingy woman, but a matter of principle. What she could not understand was why they should pay for the same services that children got for free in public schools. My father replied that this was the point, they were not the same services at all, as the teachers were more involved and the students better educated in the private schools.

"How is this discrimination possible?" my mother wondered.

"And what happens when the children finish public school? Are their chances of entering good universities the same?"

"Certainly not. This is why Irina has to go to private school."

"Is this fair?"

"What is fair is what is good for Irina. If the other parents decide differently, that's their own business."

My mother considered refusing to put me into private school as a form of protest.

"You have no right to protest," said my father angrily. "We have to accept what we find in this place. We don't have time to waste disobeying or hanging around waiting for changes. Otherwise, we're all going to suffer."

My father won the battle, as he was the one paying my tuition fees, as well as a nice amount to support my student mother. He thought that having a parent who was still going to school was a good example to follow, and that it was stimulating for me to live in such an atmosphere. When people are so wise, distance is bearable.

I never lived in luxury, though I never felt poor either, or humiliated because we didn't own a home or a car. My mother didn't drive. And when I grew up she spent one whole afternoon explaining to me why renting an apartment was much more advantageous than owning a house.

"In Canada, a house is never a big investment, mostly because houses are built of perishable materials like wood and paperboard. After 25 years, by the time you finish paying your mortgage – which is the initial sum borrowed from the bank multiplied by three because of the interest – your house isn't worth much, because it's already considered old. Besides, quite apart from the mortgage, a house is a bottomless pit. Who could possibly keep track of all the monthly expenses with the garden, the grass, flowers in the spring, irrigation in the summer, snow clearing in the winter, a tent for the car, heating, renovations? With a house, there's always something to repair or replace – the roof, the pavement, the taps, the windows, the floor, the carpet, whatever."

You understand why I do not want a house of my own. In our small family we despise people living on the outskirts, those green suburbs with tiny yards and a wooden patio where the neighbours stare at you in the swimming pool. The biggest problem with these houses is that they remove you from downtown, the kingdom of theatres, art galleries, libraries. A house in the suburbs means a life of slavery.

Like my mother, I also think that what matters is a diploma you can easily carry with you. That's freedom, as simple as that.

I went to Villa Maria, a convent that had become a Catholic school for girls. Girls from other religious groups did not have to attend the Catholic mass, just a few mandatory catechism classes. This was fine by me. I am an Orthodox Christian on my mother's side; my father and his family are atheists.

My mother had me baptized without telling my father. One Sunday morning, while I still was in diapers, my mother – accompanied by her parents – went to an Orthodox church where the priest submerged me three times in a basin full of mild water perfumed with basil leaves. Afterwards, they came back to our house for a small celebration.

My grandmother gave me a precious gift that day, a tiny cross carved out of holy wood. For the longest time, she used to insist the piece came from the cross Christ was crucified on. My mother had great difficulty convincing her that such a cross would have to have been as big as a mountain to satisfy 2000 years of Christian fervour. Afterwards, my grandmother maintained only that the wood came from Jerusalem, and that was how the cross had come to be blessed. Somewhere in the garden of Gethsemane, while waiting for his torturers, Jesus had surely touched one of those trees.

My father was told about my religion not long before he and my mother divorced, but by then it meant nothing to him. It was too late to worry about such minor things, as their quarrel went much further back. It wasn't such a big deal for my mother, either, by that time. She had never been a practicing Christian and, although she never admitted it, she was even more of an atheist than my father.

I think that being born into the Orthodox Church makes you neither too devout nor really an atheist. For my grandparents, religion was more a way of life and a bunch of superstitions. Their faith took a very tolerant form and was therefore quite acceptable. At school, I kept my religion, knowing it meant nothing as it played no role in my life. At Christmas time and Easter, my mother and I went to the Romanian church, more to get some fresh air than out of conviction.

Besides, going to church was the only way my mother kept in touch with her community. She was glad that she no longer had friends and that she didn't have to greet old acquaintances or report on her status as an eternal, jobless student. Members of her community had a good reputation with the immigration service due to the speed with which they found jobs, bought houses and went on vacations to Cuba. My mother's former fellow citizens became good Canadian citizens practically from one day to the next. They spent a great deal and got heavily into debt with their big houses and their two cars. Their philosophy of life was: "In Canada we will have everything we could not afford in our own country."

Which is why my mother appreciated not having to talk to anyone about her life. She looked like nobody except herself. She was so modest in her black coat, her knotted multi-coloured scarf, and her wool mittens. After more than 15 years, my mother belonged nowhere.

We're members of a community only as long as that community wants us, and it forces us to do what it thinks right. We belong to a group for as long as the group makes our decisions for us. An immigrant community is a sort of enlightened socialist world in which a human being dedicates himself to the community's interests while the community itself takes care of protecting us, keeping us on the right path, and giving our voice authority.

This was no longer my mother's case. Searching for a church in which to spend Christmas and Easter in the Orthodox way had nothing to do either with religion or with her community.

Before deciding which church to opt for, my mother visited all of them. For her, the main question was their membership in different patriarchies that modified the Orthodox mass. Two of them were linked to the motherland and therefore submitted to the Patriarch of Bucharest: the two others were loyal to the Patriarch Nathanael, based in Chicago, a kind of dissident church born in the aftermath of the Second World War when the Communists came to power and there was a massive exodus of Orthodox Russians, Romanians, Serbs, and Bulgarians.

My mother did not sympathize with those dissident churches, which had shortened the mass to cater to Americanized Orthodox believers. She did not like progressive priests who softened the harsh Byzantine canon and flouted the old Orthodox rules. One example being that a priest had to marry a virgin and was certainly not allowed to marry a divorced woman, as had happened in one instance.

Personally, I think the main reason for her discontent was aesthetic. When Orthodox missions lacked the money to build their own churches, they usually rented other Christian churches from Catholics or Protestants. My mother found this hybridization repugnant. What she especially disapproved of was the absence of the iconostasis, a kind of wall covered with orthodox icons that is supposed to keep the priest hidden from view during mass. The metamorphosis of the bread and the wine had to be kept from ordinary mortals' comprehension and sight, and remain as secret as the Eleusinian mysteries,

After two years of searching, my mother had narrowed her search down to two Romanian missions that had succeeded in building their own Orthodox churches. The bigger of the two was on Christophe-Colombe Street, led since the 1950s by an authoritarian priest with a repu-

tation of having been an ultranationalist Legionary parti-
san. My mother disliked his tyrannical way of conducting
the business of the church and his secret involvement in
community quarrels.

One Easter evening, my mother finally decided on the
church on Masson Street, a colourful wooden building with
a huge iconostasis covered in icons donated by community
artists, and topped by a starry blue ceiling. People said the
old priest had been a spy for the Romanian Secret Service
before the fall of the Communist regime. The money used
to build the church had been donated by the Romanian Pa-
triarchy, so how could you not suspect that the Secret Service was involved? Where else could this sudden interest in
the Diaspora have come from, given that monasteries and
churches were being toppled at the time in Romania itself?

On the night of Resurrection, when my mother made
up her mind, the mass was dreadfully long, respecting all
the old Orthodox rules. Four hours of religious songs, in-
cense, and prayers! My mother thought this right, since we
had travelled such a long way to attend the service. The
choir was run by professionals trained in theological insti-
tutes, and she was especially pleased that all the choristers
were men. But what convinced my mother to remain faithful to this particular church was that, at the end, the priest
gave us each a small glass of wine with some bread, the
flesh and the blood of Christ. This was unexpected; the
other missions gave people breadcrumbs, which appalled
my mother. How dare they disgrace The Last Supper
when – the Bible was explicit on this matter – the Lord had
poured his blood into his disciple's glasses?

So my mother stopped roaming and settled on this
church. She went only at Christmas and Easter, and for a
few years I accompanied her. Later on, I refused to go, and
my mother, uncomfortable about crossing the city alone at
midnight, also stopped going.

All of which is to say that I remain an Orthodox Christian. At Villa Maria my religion did not bother me, and as long as it was not embarrassing, why would I want to change it? I attended the Catholic mass and sang in the church choir.

The reason I've been talking about my religion is that Yannis, as a Greek, was Orthodox, too. Right from the beginning of our relationship, that seemed like a sign to me. His name was Greek for John, and St. John was the one who paved the way to the Messiah. He was a baptizer despite himself, but I will not take this any further.

I was talking about my time at Villa Maria.

On the school's centenary, the Archbishop made a speech that included a definition of Catholicism later printed in our school paper: "Coming from the Greek, Catholic means universal. Your school is universal because it is open towards the big wide world. It is universal because it welcomes young people from all cultures and religions. It is universal because it refers to Jesus's teachings on what we consider today to be the civilization of love. Only someone who does not truly understand Catholicism would be ashamed of it?"

I was touched by this Catholic education that made me familiar with religious matters. I have a better understanding today of why Catholics have so much trouble getting rid of the totalitarian universe of their faith. Their love for the Lord is strongly tied to a holy atmosphere carefully created over many centuries. The paintings, the extravagant architecture, the magnificent music, all play an important role in keeping the faith alive. When a Catholic loses his faith, he is banished from a beautiful place, a kind of an antechamber to heaven. Unfortunately, those who get rid of God do not drop their secret hope that Paradise still exists.

In my little Orthodox family, the love of God comes and goes easily, according to circumstances and our mood. As for the holy atmosphere, priests in Canada preferred to rent Anglican or Baptist buildings because they were smaller. The worst, however, according to my mother, was an Orthodox mass in a deserted Catholic cathedral with clerics who closed their eyes to this sacrilege in order to pay the heating bills. That was one way to deny the past and reconcile two religions that continue their age-old conflict over a few words – and that had chosen to miss out on every chance they had to get along. An Orthodox mass performed in a Catholic church was not just strange; it was blasphemy.

One morning after I got the second letter from Yannis, I woke up thinking about the Archbishop's speech, but not because of his view of Catholicism. There was another passage in which he mentioned a woman's comments about men going to war. What had struck me at the time was that the Archbishop said this woman was a Jew. Why didn't he say just that it was a woman – a wife or a mother torn apart by the distress of seeing her husband or son facing death? This was the question I asked myself: Why did he specify that she was Jewish?

Still in my pajamas, I asked my mother to help me find the box with my old school stuff, for she had saved all of it.

"This is our only heritage," she had said at the time. "It doesn't mean anything to you yet, but for your children it will." For those who arrive with their entire fortune packed into two suitcases, children's memories are all that matter.

My mother helped me find the box without asking why.

Since Yannis had come into my life, she probably thought everything I did concerned him in one way or another.

I quickly found the bulletin with the photograph of the Archbishop in front of the school chapel. And there was the passage I was looking for: "I have been struck by some lines written by a Jewish woman called Lilly. She said that as long as women refuse to come out onto the world stage, the world will be mutilated. The first value women will bring to the world will be peace. How can a woman let the man she loves or her son go to war? Women know what life is because they create it."

My best friend at Villa Maria was Marika, whose parents were Dutch. Right from the beginning, an unconscious intimacy was established between us, what Goethe called an elective affinity. I don't know much about this kind of friendship between girls, but this was what we surely both experienced: an elective affinity. Young people are more aware than adults who their best friends are, and they always make the right choice. I have never had such a good relationship since with anyone of my age and gender.

Later on, after continuing her studies at Brébeuf, Marika enrolled in an architecture program in Amsterdam, where her parents went back to live after their retirement. Her departure was another reason for me not to respond to my classmates' invitations. It would have been more difficult to refuse Marika. I was able to get out of invitations from others easily enough. My mother had taken that story of the cold sore from me, but my old classmates were less cunning than her friend the writer, and they always believed me.

What particularly tied me to Marika were the religious plays she and I used to stage in her basement about the first religious mission to Montreal. Along with a few Chinese classmates, we used to recreate the days when about

fifty French men and women came to live in New France
to build the mystical city of Marie — Ville Marie or Villa
Maria.

I think I should tell you more about these plays, for
they were what I loved most in my high school years.

Marika lived in a nice house not far from the school,
and we went there to play those brave men and women who
were guided by faith and led by the soldier Paul Chomedey,
Sieur de Maisonneuve, and by the nurse Jeanne Mance.

Because of her tennis training and her stature, Marika took some of the male roles, and I played some of the
women. She was Maisonneuve, and I was Jeanne Mance.
We cut our costumes out of old curtains we found in her
mother's storeroom. For the rosaries, we ruined an antique
wooden-beaded abacus that her mother used to keep on
the mantelpiece.

So every Saturday afternoon we played those devout
Christians, keepers of the faith that was to crumble in the
Old World because of bloody conflicts between Catholics
and Huguenots. New France would reinvigorate Catholicism, this universal religion — as the Archbishop would have
it — open towards the whole world, and create a civilization
of love. A free life, without fear and without danger, was to
be established in the small Indian village of Hochelaga on
the island of Montreal.

Our religious theatre focused on the period between
the arrival of the settlers, in 1642, and the abandonment
of the fort, in 1683. Set design demanded some ingenu-
ity, for we needed to recreate a point between on the St.
Lawrence River. What helped was a visit organized by our
school to the Pointe-à-Callière Museum, which had apparently been built on the ruins of the old Ville Marie fort.
From this base on the shores of the St. Lawrence, people
could keep one eye on the river and the other on the slopes

of Mont Royal, where the Indians were hiding.

For the location of the fort, we relied on rough draw-
ings that researchers from McGill had found somewhere
in the United States. The map sketched by royal engineer
Jean Bourdon shows a few buildings – the governor's house,
other residences, a shop, a chapel, a forge and a kitchen –
clustered around an armory. During recent excavations ar-
cheologists have found the remnants of a well and a large
oven, surrounded by a pile of ashes and the bones of vari-
ous animals. This was likely where the first settlers butch-
ered game and cooked it. The oven was linked to a sewage
pit by a corridor also used as a sanitary chute. In the same
spot they also found handicrafts, gun stones, pipes, French
pottery, Indian tools, and ceramic beads used for trading.

Since our plays went back to very beginnings of the
city of Montreal, we began with Jérôme Le Royer de La
Dauversière and the first steps towards creating what would
become the Société Notre-Dame de Montréal. Le Royer
had been educated by the Jesuits, though they doubted the
sincerity of his faith. Nobody could deny that the Montreal
enterprise was the fruit of his feverish activity.

Marika portrayed him as a plump country gentleman,
as we wanted to make fun of the man who campaigned for
the Christianization of lands he never set foot on and that
he only knew from stories circulated by the Jesuits. We imagined that his religious fervour had little in common with
faith, although there is some evidence that he was devout.

Here he is knocking on the nobles' doors, welcomed
by the gracious hostesses, and making an effort to convince
them of the need to implant a piece of France among the
natives; educate them, get them to kneel before the Cross,
leave their smelly huts for proper houses, and put an end to
the sin in which they lived.

Unfortunately, this good man was not wealthy. A poor

manager with a big family to feed, he was unable to hold on to his capital, let alone increase it. His strength was in persuasion, and he eventually found a wealthy associate, Pierre Chevrier, Baron de Fancamp, who agreed to finance this noble enterprise. After long negotiations between the Church and the royal court, they were granted the island of Montreal on December 17, 1640.

Why did they insist on Montreal, where no French settler was living at the time? Why this passion for a no man's land traveled by the Algonquin people and periodically besieged by their sworn enemies, the Agniers?

From a military point of view, Montreal had no importance as a colony; in the war between the Indian tribes, the island was dangerously exposed and would be the first place to fall. Economic considerations were clearly unimportant to Le Royer and de Chevrier, and it was widely known by that time that the Silk Road did not cross the Canadian prairies.

Embarrassing as it may seem today, what interested them was simply the apostolic goal. They saw the island of Montreal as the New Jerusalem for which they were ready to set up a new Crusade. From their comfortable homes, they dreamed of reuniting the Indian hunters and gathering them into a Christian community.

The departure from New France of the three missionary ships in 1639 had a big impact in France. The first recruitment consisted of 37 men sailing in two convoys leaving from La Rochelle and Dieppe.

On one vessel was Paul Chomedey, Sieur de Maisonneuve, to whom Le Royer had entrusted the expedition. A career soldier aged 29, he asked for nothing better than to put himself at the service of God, King and the New

World missionaries.

Paul had been born into an impoverished noble family in 1612 in Neuville-sur-Vanne, in the Champagne region. For young man in his position, the army offered the best chance of making a modest fortune. At 14, he enrolled in the Dutch army, which was the only one waging war in Europe at the time. The horrors he experienced on the battlefield distressed him, however. When he got back home, he tried to forget the terrors that haunted his nights by spending his time reading works of philosophy and poetry. These solitary hours transformed him into a lonely and dreamy person.

A book we found in the school library showed portraits of Paul and Jeanne at the time they left for the New World. Paul's face is long and flat, with a fringe cut above the forehead, a strong nose, and a protruding chin that was apparently a feature common to people in Champagne.

Jeanne has the same kind of nose, but her small chin and her big eyes give her a very fragile look. The tiny oil painting that is signed by Dugardin along with an inscription reading, "True portrait of Mademoiselle Mance before she came to Canada in 1638" is preserved in the Archives of *Les soeurs hospitalières de Montréal*. Jeanne is dressed in the bourgeois style, her curly hair tucked under the veil that frames her pleasant face. This picture was quite different from the one hanging in our school library, which showed Jeanne with a rounder face, and a dark cape concealing her shoulders.

Among Paul's entourage in Champagne, people were talking more and more about the Canadian mission. But how could he tell his father that he was going to leave the family and that he had no intention of getting married, having children or running the ancestral property? How could he explain why he wanted to sail on one of those rickety ships and live next to naked cannibals in the name of a faith that, much like the French fleet, was in danger of sinking around them?

Paul had no choice but to lie to his father about the aim of this journey. He persuaded his father of the rightness of his decision by talking about material gain rather than about religious aims. He told wonderful stories about huge fortunes amassed from nothing, and this eventually convinced his father to give Paul his blessing. If the gentleman was insensitive to lofty ideals, he apparently had no argument with the prospect of wealth.

So Paul boarded a ship bound for Canada along with 25 other men. Le Royer had unhesitatingly assigned him the mission of the Notre Dame Society, whose apostolic aim was to convert the Indian peoples of New France. On board with him, Paul took a sword and a few books, including Descartes' *Discourse on the Method*, which was the one he valued most.

Jeanne Mance left at the same time on another vessel. It was at this point in the story that I moved on stage as this bourgeois woman, while Marika moved out of the role of Le Royer and donned Maisonneuve's cape.

Jeanne had been born in 1601, and she took her vow of chastity at the age of seven. When she was 17, her mother passed away, leaving Jeanne in charge of a household of 12 children. In 1631, her father's death left her as the sole support of her sisters and brothers. She studied with the Ursulines, showing a special vocation early on for charitable work, and she devoted herself to the care of the sick during the plague that devastated La Rochelle in 1637.

One day, her routine was disrupted when her cousin, Nicolas Dolebeau, who was a Jesuit, told her stories about Canada. What interested her most was the discovery that, in New France, women were for the first time allowed to take part in a religious mission to foreign lands. Her cousin also told her about the enthusiasm created in Paris by a visit from Madame de la Peltrie and Marie de l'Incarnation, two missionaries from Canada who had returned to solicit funding from the French aristocracy to help build a hospital in Quebec.

Jeanne Mance was enthralled. If women were permitted to help get this terra incognita converted to Christianity, might she herself not be one of those skirted apostles? By 1640, Jeanne was free of responsibility. Despite fragile health, she signed up for the Montreal mission.

She travelled from La Rochelle to Quebec with the Jesuit Père La Place and 12 workers. Beside Jeanne, there were three more women bound for Montreal, the wives of craftsmen who had refused to go without their families. This was allowed because it had proved very difficult to recruit settlers skilled as carpenters, joiners, masons and blacksmiths. Also needed were forestry and sawmill workers, people to clear the land, sailors and soldiers, a surgeon and a gunsmith. With the few exceptions mentioned above, the 1641 immigrants were almost all single men.

The winter of 1641 passed desperately slowly in Quebec. Paul in particular had difficulty getting used to the harshness of the climate. His attempts to use snowshoes to move from one place to another were the laughing stock of the settlers, as he often stumbled and fell. Besides, in the small colony he and Jeanne were more and more often being referred to as "two young fools."

In spring, as soon as conditions allowed, the vessels built in Quebec over the winter were loaded with food supplies, tools and wood. Forty-four people boarded four small boats to go upstream. There are no written accounts of the journey; no one wrote down their first impressions, fears or uncertainties. The passengers were on their guard, too worried about arrows to think of writing. Towards the end of her life, though, Jeanne told people that during this journey she had seen beautiful lands dotted with colourful flowers.

The boats dropped anchor in Montreal on May 17, 1642. After unloading, the men put up tents as protection against rain and cold. The next day the settlers all attended the first religious service on the island. They erected a small altar, and Jeanne decorated it with flowers. Dressed in his liturgical vestments, Père Vimont struck up Veni Creator. During the sermon, according to some witnesses, he said, "We owe our resources to France, thanks to the generosity and kindness of a few men and especially their wives." Which is an acknowledgement that Montreal owes its existence to the charity of women.

Master carpenters and joiners started building houses right away. In 1642, a small fortification surrounded a church and some log cabins. Jeanne Mance organized the first clinic in Montreal in one of the huts. The Indians and their families started coming to the camp asking to be baptized. In return, they got a piece of land where they could settle. Maisonneuve and Jeanne became godfather and godmother to little dark-skinned Josephs, Pierres, and Maries.

Two years later, the settlers left their log cabins for more comfortable and solid houses. The hospital Jeanne had dreamed of was built outside the fort, and Jeanne moved in before it was finished. The building was equipped with a tiny kitchen, a room for herself and another one for patients. She was the first person to leave the fort and live alone in the forest with her assistant, Catherine Lézeau, a few acres from the Montreal community.

It was a challenge to adjust to life in Ville Marie, which

had a very different feel from France.

In summer, the settlers' skin suffered from mosquitoes and other huge and virulent insects. In winter, the bread and wine froze on the table in the refectory. Snow snuck in through cracks in the walls.

The biggest challenge for the settlers was to adapt their clothing to the harsh weather. Jeanne Mance dressed all the women in clothes made from beaver leather, sewing together two pieces of fur the way the Indians did. Paul often made fun of the nuns' outfits and headdresses, which were so faded and threadbare that you had no way of knowing either the colour or the fabric.

The Notre Dame Society sent supplies of livestock, cereal, and furniture from France. A later convoy brought what the settlers needed most – other human beings – on a vessel sent personally by Louis XIII. The ship was called *Notre Dame*, and its precious freight included ammunition and the invaluable gift of an agronomist and a military engineer. These were the contribution of Queen Anne of Austria, a fervent Catholic and supporter of the Montreal cause. This was encouraging, but the number of believers would soon diminish considerably, and it wasn't long before the missionaries were left to themselves – and to the hardships of the country.

In 1644, Maisonneuve was named Governor of Montreal. He received the precious document in the presence of Jeanne, who was surely impressed by the honour bestowed on her companion in faith. Construction soon began on the Governor's House not far from the hospital, on a windmill, and on a bigger graveyard. Little by little, the improvised fortress, though still modest and provisional, was taking on the style of a European settlement.

Paul and Jeanne's dream did not last long. The settlers, who had survived thanks to the generosity of the Notre Dame Society in France, came to realize that the colony would have to come to terms with trade, bigger buildings, roads, and adventurers. The appearance of commercial shops and even a ministry of religion started to corrupt Paul and Jeanne's vision of a peaceful and natural existence.

No apostolic aim can remain aloof from commercial interest. Faith can never exist outside the institutions that protect it and, eventually, transform it into a weapon. The new colony was therefore obliged to increase the number of its residences and to welcome newcomers from Quebec and Trois-Rivières. On the other side of the ocean, the Notre Dame Society desperately needed to reform its own finances, for it had neither capital nor income, and enthusiasm had started to cool.

Even when we weren't rehearsing, Marika and I thought a lot about the brave men and women linked together in a genuine congregation, where people called each other sister and brother, where rules were unwritten, and where there were neither records nor savings accounts. Our plays dwelled on the settlers' daily activities, which consisted of praying and working hard to maintain and expand the community. Sometimes they also had to become soldiers to drive back some of the Indian tribes.

In 1647, the settlers were granted a small plot of land in their names as well as the right to trade furs with the Indians. The only person indifferent to this was Maisonneuve. As Governor, he was owed a small percentage of the settlers' profits for his subsistence, but he often forfeited what was his in attempts to resolve conflicts and difficulties among his men. In one case, the tailor Guillaume Chartier, the poorest of the settlers, was unable to trade with the Indians as he had nothing to offer them in exchange for their pelts. Maisonneuve gave him the curtains from his own house so that Chartier could make clothes and pay the Indians.

The period between 1648 and 1653 was troubled. The conflict between the Huron and the Iroquois erupted into violence that threatened the security of Ville Marie. The settlers were so frightened that they packed their bags and boarded the first vessel bound for France. Jeanne Mance then decided to make the biggest sacrifice in her power. With the situation so radically changed, and security more important than anything else, she handed over to Maisonneuve the funds — 22,000 pounds — that their benefactor Madame de Bullion had donated for the hospital.

Paul set off for France to recruit soldiers and purchase ammunition. He ended up staying in France for two years, longer than expected, because he had to comfort his sister Jacqueline, whose husband had been murdered by a cousin. Paul struggled to help her in this crisis, but in vain, for the workings of the French bureaucracy — unlike those of the Montreal settlement — were out of his control. The cousin remained free and unpunished, and four years later murdered Jacqueline herself.

When Maisonneuve returned to Montreal in 1652, he brought 120 men and 30 women with him and was greeted by the settlers on the shores of the St. Lawrence. For Jeanne, Paul had another present: a young nun called Marguerite Bourgeoys. Jeanne herself was never a nun, just a secular nurse who would later become the manager of the hospital. However, Jeanne would have good relations with the religious women around her, and especially with Marguerite.

Between 1653 and 1659 the colony took on new life, as the soldiers were able to safeguard its security so the settlers could dedicate themselves to their work in the fields. They cleared new land, ploughed, seeded, built bigger houses, and set up a flourishing business with the Indians, who controlled the impenetrable forests into the continent.

There was no peace for Maisonneuve, however. In

1655, he had to go back to France for Jacqueline's burial and the settling of her estate. Again he was away for two years, but he kept in close touch with Ville Marie. When he returned, he brought with him four priests from the Order of Saint-Sulpice, which was less strict than the Jesuit Order.

In 1658, it was Jeanne's turn to voyage to France in search of more money and new settlers. The journey was made at great personal cost, for she had fallen on the ice and broken her forearm in two places and dislocated her wrist. Almost incapable of moving, this generous woman nevertheless decided to return to France, wanting to carry out this last service for the mission before she died. She left Quebec in October.

On her arrival at La Rochelle, she insisted on going on to La Flèche at once to pay a visit to the settlement's spiritual leader and benefactor, Le Royer. She made the entire journey on a stretcher carried by four men, for she could not stand the jolts of travelling in a vehicle. Le Royer received her coldly; he himself was sick and ill-tempered. As Jeanne had long suspected, her patron was lacking not only management skills but faith, as well.

She set off again for Paris to visit Madame de Bullion. Miraculously, after a few days on the road, she started to feel better, declaring herself completely healed by the time she got to Paris. Her dramatic recovery caused a sensation, and Jeanne knew how to take advantage of her sudden fame to promote the Montreal cause among the wealthy and pious women. Madame de Bullion donated another 20,000 pounds that Jeanne personally brought back to Ville Marie.

Le Royer's death, the following year, marked the ruin of the Notre Dame Society, which in 1663 was obliged to sell Montreal to the Sulpicians to settle its debts. The coronation of King Louis XIV further changed the rules of the game when Montreal and Quebec came under the jurisdiction of a single Sovereign Council.

Maisonneuve refused to accept the authority of the Governor of Quebec. Montreal was his island, and he would not give it up. Quebec therefore organized a blockade of supplies destined for Montreal. Maisonneuve was relieved of his duties and sent back to France. The colony came under royal administration, which knew nothing about the life of the settlement.

After the departure of her friend and protector, Jeanne's life was little more than a painful expectation of death. Her role at the hospital had diminished. Old friends were disappearing one by one. But nothing was as unbearable for Jeanne as the pain caused by Monseigneur de Laval, Bishop of Quebec.

Irritated by Montreal's independence, Laval did not like the idea of a religious colony ruled by secular people, and he never accepted the fact that France owed the existence of Montreal to the devotion of a soldier and a nurse. After Maisonneuve's departure, Laval hounded Jeanne, insisting she repay back the money Madame de Buillon had given her for the hospital, the original 22,000 pounds the nurse had given to Maisonneuve to buy an army and protect the fort. From Paris, Maisonneuve did everything in his power to protect Jeanne, but in vain. The Bishop pursued legal proceedings against the old woman.

Apart from her personal grieving, Jeanne was pained to see what the settlement had become. Montreal was going through a bad period, and traffic in alcohol and guns had undermined the early settlers' tranquility and confidence.

Jeanne Mance died on June 18, 1673, at the age of 70. Her heart was put in an iron box and set in the small Hotel Dieu chapel under the lamp of Saint Sacrament. Unfortunately, a fire in the chapel reduced it to ashes before it could be moved into the new church.

Our religious plays about Paul and Jeanne in Montreal are almost all I can tell you about my childhood. The rest can be summarized in a few sentences. I can't have much of a memory, if my entire childhood is reduced to my years at Villa Maria. What I still remember are my frozen legs, as our uniform consisted of a shirt, a blue sweater and a kilt up above our knees. I recall hurrying to get indoors at the métro to escape the cruel winds.

Maybe I should mention Open House at the beginning of the school year, when I was assigned to the science laboratory to show new recruits and their parents an electrical engine. To test the electric current, visitors had to touch a big iron ball, and it was my job to tell them not to be alarmed, even though I knew that the power produced was not only strong, but amplified by their fear and surprise.

Marika was in the biology laboratory, where her role was to dissect a pig embryo in front of visitors and demonstrate its internal organs. She used the same fetus all day long, washed in alcohol so that it wouldn't stink in the overcrowded room. When the room was empty, Marika played with the animal's tiny organs, passing her gloved hands over the little heart muscles and the spongy lungs.

Marika was my one and only friend. A woman does not have more than one real friend in her life, and when that friendship comes to an end there will never be another. When Marika and I parted, we knew it was forever, and that it was not even worth keeping track of each other. After a while, we found out how vulnerable friendship is at this age.

On the other hand, it is true that real friendships can only be forged at this age. Older people never experience this feeling of complete communion with someone, such fear of loss and loneliness. Children's experiences of these strong feelings are, I think, a counterweight to their animal-like selfishness. Childhood is a combination of insane cruelty and supreme altruism.

So Marika's departure healed me of feminine friendships. I have always had a lot of acquaintances among my classmates, as I always had an ability to make friends, but I would never again play nurse and soldier or build a mystical city on an island. I would never again experience that strange mixture of atheistic indifference and religious enthusiasm. Marika and I understood that people could avoid God, but not faith. She had always envied me the role I played in our theatre, and often told me I had a vocation as a healer. Later on, she convinced herself that Maisonneuve's character was not out of line with her life either. She, too, was an explorer. She still travels a lot, but I don't know anything else about her. Maybe she is searching for her Jeanne Mance self, while I am looking for my own Paul Chomedey de Maisonneuve.

It's time to get back to the story of the photograph.

Two weeks after the incident on campus, my mother – who knew about the photograph – came home with the magazine that had my face on the cover. She had bought two copies. We left the magazine on the small table in the sitting room to look at while we smoked our cigarettes. Inside there was a long piece on the university rankings, but neither of us read it.

By next day, I was a celebrity. It started in class, where I felt what it's like to be noticed when you enter a room. My classmates and professors, even people from other departments, stared at me in the halls. I felt people's eyes on me when I was sipping coffee and eating my favourite blueberry muffin in the cafeteria. I felt proud of this without knowing exactly what I had done to deserve it. It was just fate that had played into my hands, but there are always people who think that anyone who had been lucky must be worthy of attention.

I hope it's obvious that I am not someone who gets drunk on cold water. This cover photo did not change my life. It would not give me everything I had always lacked. If you were to ask me what I didn't have or what I had always longed for, I would in any case have great difficulty telling you.

As you can tell, I am not wealthy at all, and I have no way of knowing if my diploma will allow me to get a better job when I get my Master's degree. Becoming a rival to Paris Hilton all of a sudden was not something that made me shiver with pleasure. So I did not really understand the excessive attention my classmates were now paying me. The truth is that their interest was no more than a little envy mixed up with nastiness and the hidden desire that this incident be forgotten as soon as possible. I know this because I would have felt the same thing. It's like winning a small amount on the lottery: it has no fundamental effect on your life.

I have to admit, though, that a strange sensation came over me in class when I caught people eyeing me. The more I noticed their stares, the more confidence I gained in myself. Once more, I have to say that I am not naïve, or overly naïve. But I can assure you that people never know the truth about themselves and, particularly not about their physical appearance.

I was too used to my face to find anything new there. I knew I was not bad looking, but I wasn't slaying people on every street corner, either. But that cover picture revealed to me my own beauty, buried in the grave of lifelong habits, muddied by the routine that makes us ordinary to ourselves.

It was the same sensation I experienced on a beach,

watching the surface of the water on a calm summer day. Everything was smooth, when suddenly a wave came out of the depths to break on the shore with a small sound. How could this happen? A moment of absent-mindedness and the eye would have missed the instant when the surface of the water folded into a small pleat that grew and grew as it drew closer to the shore.

I felt like this kind of wave, just part of the mass of water in the sea for so long, and now suddenly here I was with my very own existence. Exposed to the scrutiny of other people, I was no longer anonymous. My oval face was perfectly divided between the height of the forehead, the protuberant chin, and the nose, which perfectly matched my Mongol eyes.

I did not know this face. The photographer had immortalized it through an angle and in an attitude that perfectly expressed my usual mood – a hint of fatigue, indifference and nonchalance. I am not talking about any qualities of my own, but in the photograph that combination lent me an unearthly dignity. Even my mother looked at me with different eyes. She was detaching herself from me, her child. I was blossoming. I did not belong to her anymore.

The awareness of your own beauty changes you into another person, for beauty, whatever people say, is always a big asset. The number of gorgeous women who have a good life is incredible, especially when compared to the lives of intelligent women. Under the admiring gaze of my classmates, I was becoming someone I could trust.

Two weeks later, I was still enjoying this boost to my self-esteem, in spite of the fact that my mother had put the magazine out of sight on the highest shelf in the apartment. By the time Pierre got home, she would have forgotten the incident and neglect to show him my picture. You can see how inconvenient it is not to have a big family, friends, and good neighbours. My mother had nobody to talk to about my achievements. As for my father, she had no intention at all of calling him to inform him about my new status as cover girl.

We were therefore about to forget the incident when the phone rang one day. It was my mother who answered, as I was not at home. That evening, she told me that some-body from *Maclear's* had called because there was a letter for me from Afghanistan in the new issue.

Afghanistan? I could not believe my ears. Who could possibly be writing to me from Afghanistan?

It was a Canadian soldier, my mother explained curtly. She had started to feel afraid. What was this all about? How could you trust the media? And what was going to happen? Her fear amused me, especially as she was the one who gave the caller my email. In time, this would look to her like a terrible betrayal.

The following day, in class, everybody knew about this letter. They did not get the information from the magazine, which came out at the beginning of the week, but from one of the big newspapers that had heard the news and was now spreading it under the appealing title, "The Darling of Kandahar." Somebody showed the article to me and at lunchtime I went to buy a copy of *Maclear's* for my mother.

On the second page, in the Mail Bag section, there was a letter that seemed to me addressed to the magazine:

> I am writing this letter from my checkpoint, looking forward to getting off duty, and looking at this girl who is playfully watching me from the cover of your maga-zine. She's the best thing I have to look at here. Ever since I've been deployed to operations in Afghanistan, Maclear's has become my preferred source for Ca-

nadian news. Here in the desert, people read a wide range of material, including Playboy, which does not excite anyone because everything in it is so superficial and overdone. However, since my lads have seen this issue, they've all been impressed with the young lady's natural beauty and incredible sexiness. The whole garrison agrees that she is the best pin-up in our collection. You've made me very happy with this refreshing image, so I wonder if it is possible to thank this girl on my behalf for being who she is. I won't hide from you that I badly want to know her name.

The letter was signed by Corporal Yannis Alexandridis of the Second Battalion, Royal Canadian Regiment.

After the break, I found on my desk a piece of paper with these words on it: "For the sexiest girl in Afghanistan." One of my classmates, an Argentine student working on Borges, admitted that he was the culprit. This foolishness surprised me, coming from Fernando who had always been Borges's watchdog, defending him tooth and nail.

To understand what I am talking about, you should know that while Borges remains a major figure in world literature, his star had faded in our department. This is because of one of our professors, who is of Polish origin – and don't not forget that Poland is the motherland of Witold Gombrowicz, the writer who in his novel *Trans-Atlantyk* makes fun of Borges (named Cortez in the novel) and his habit of traveling everywhere with a coterie of fans.

One day, when Fernando was quoting Borges for the umpteenth time, this professor asked him: "My dear friend, could you explain to me why Borges had to dedicate an ode to Peron after the latter had appointed him head of the national library? I know it was his dearest dream to be a librarian, but did he really need to lick the boots of such a dictator?"

I don't remember Fernando's answer, but his venera-
tion for the blind poet was unshaken. The fact that Fernando was able to come down from the tower where he was
keeping an eye on Borges's reputation to write me a snide
note surprised us all.

I sometimes had a strange vision of my classmates as
they sat behind their desks, stuck to their chairs, with only
the upper part of their body visible. I used to imagine they
were all turning into monsters, half-human, half-object,
their fleshy torsos living on a wooden bottom. I would see
these human-objects leaving the room carrying out this
square body, walking on four iron feet, wearing four plastic
corks to stifle the creaking of the floor.

Now it was their turn to judge me, to imagine me
barely dressed, singing and dancing on an improvised stage
in front of the Canadian troops in Kandahar, a latter-day
Marilyn being hooted at by soldiers.

The most scathing was Serguei, a young Russian recently landed on Canadian soil who had not yet learned
the finer points of political correctness. When one of our
classmates from Senegal came to school one day all dressed
in white, he even said, "Yédidya, look at you! You've become white!" He now advised me to focus on classical Afghan literature, as the long civil wars had not allowed the
arts to develop recently.

"You should know," an Armenian classmate retorted,
"given the length of time the Russian army spent in Afghanistan."

It was strange to see how even literature can become a
battlefield. People don't only fight for bread and water but
for ideas too. This is the terrible difference between human beings and animals. There were 20 of us in my M.A.
group, and almost everyone represented and defended a

different part of the world. For most, the department was a transit stop between their native country and the new one. Before trying something else, young people with a literary background land in schools for three main reasons: to improve their language, to transfer their diplomas, and to get scholarships, which are sometimes their only income.

They all liked to believe that universities are the democratic environment *par excellence*, places where it was possible to make a smooth transition to another language and culture. When they spoke, they all had their native accents and made their own grammatical mistakes. At the outset, their origins seemed of no importance, but after just one semester they had sorted themselves into groups from different regions, remembering old conflicts between their forefathers. After the second semester, their friendships with their fellow students – and their antipathies – were no different from those of their own people. In their new country, they carried on old national adversities as if they were back at home. This country was not multicultural enough to allow them to forget their parents' suffering and humiliation.

What now? I had felt so good at school, and suddenly everything seemed so politicized to me. Unlike the working environment, in universities people still trust the politicians' good will and the fairness of multiculturalism. Thanks to the huge number of classes on racism, colonialism, and hyphenated-identities, we thought it possible to take the theory from university out into the street and apply it to ordinary people.

In our classroom, the most interesting people were the non-Americans and the non-Europeans, that is to say the Others. Bearers of two cultures, familiar with two different social, political and religious systems, we thought they were more tolerant and more comprehensive. It was their mission to make it possible for our two worlds, East and West, to join; it was their job to annihilate the Eurocentric discourse that was so old it had become annoying. These new figures were fresh.

We were taught to be ashamed of the racism and discrimination that our parents and grandparents had perpetrated against their kin. Now, finally we could speak freely about issues such as the Jews and the Holocaust, the extermination of the First Nations in the interests of democracy, faith and fundamentalism. All the Others had to be known in their doubleness and their non-domestic identity. We no longer dared to raise issues of difference or specificity, because that supposed we were still dividing the world up into a centre and its multiple peripheries. We all agreed we should finally give the Others the right to express their needs as they wished, and to represent themselves and their identity in their own way.

This made me understand, nevertheless, that even at university differences remain the same outside the amphitheatres, as cut off from the life and the noise of the street as a prison. Great ideas were swarming around, certainly, but it would take time for them to break through the thick concrete walls. Almighty multiculturalism was no more than a political slogan, which often took hilarious, absurd, turns. All we hoped was that in the future it would breed real change. If the form has already been set, one day the contents would follow.

My case reawakened some of these old adversities. But I decided neither to get angry nor to feel hurt. I was famous for a reason that did not touch me particularly, and one I had done nothing to deserve. Here I was faced with a big dilemma: what does an individual wish for most in his life? Or, to put it more simply: what had I hoped to achieve through my existence? Had I ever had aspirations that went beyond our neighbourhood, the house I lived in, or my mother's personal example? Money, men, love? What had really excited me in the years since I embodied Jeanne Mance?

The sad reality was that I could not think of anything, so perhaps I have never had big aspirations. Marika was right. I had a vocation for being a nurse. Nevertheless, even Jeanne Mance, a humble woman dedicated to the sick, ended up having a street and also a park named after her in the mystical city for which she worked all her life.

Fame is annoying when you did not struggle for it and you never even dreamt about it. Fame is good when you have a lot of friends and a big family interested in your career and impressed by your achievements. When you live anonymously, fame is just a nuisance. I understood that the same evening, at work, when I was tying on my green apron and about to enter the room where the noise of the customers was growing. I forgot to tell you that I work at Les Trois Brasseurs, which I hate because of the peanut shells that everybody thinks they're allowed to spill all over the floor. The crack of broken shells underfoot drives me crazy.

Of all the small jobs I've had as a student, though, this was the least annoying, even if it was also the most exhausting. What I find hard with jobs is the repetitiveness of small, mechanical gestures. Monotony drives me mad. I am talking about the work I did for two manufacturers. The first was a toy company where I had to match small kitchen utensils and box them. The second was a small family business producing jewelry boxes. That was where I met my second lover, Manuel.

So, at present, I am working at Les Trois Brasseurs on St. Denis, on the corner of de Maisonneuve, not far from UQÀM and the Cinémathèque. Apart from students, the customers are people who read all kinds of stuff – people who might well, in other words, have seen my picture on the cover of *Maclear's* magazine.

No one made any comment, however. The week the issue was released, not a single customer had seen the cover. It was the letter sent by Yannis that caught one man's attention, as under the text they had reprinted a small copy of my picture with the mortarboard on my head. It was probably somebody who, less drunk than usual, had noticed the likeness between the image and the first floor waitress. The same person must have shown the picture to one of the guys behind the bar and commented on the resemblance.

I wasn't working that day, but my fame among the other waitresses increased all the same. Someone had the idea of putting the article up in the restaurant. The next day, when I went to work, I saw my picture pinned up at the main entrance, above the menu. At the beginning, this meant nothing to me, and the attention I got from a few customers, which was fine, convinced me to leave the article in its place. Why not?

From the next day onwards, I was acting again, for the second time in my life. This time, I was playing myself, a woman loved by a whole regiment of Canadian soldiers and the best thing that had happened to young men fighting for justice in Afghanistan. At the end of his letter, Yannis told the magazine to thank me for what I was. But finally, who was I? I did not know myself well enough to be happy with that.

The new issue of *Maclear's* might help me to find out.

That same week, a team from *Maclear's* came in and asked for me while I was on my shift. The photographer I knew by name, Kevin, was accompanied by a journalist whose face vaguely resembled that of the woman on the six o'clock news, though there was in fact no connection between them. They had my whereabouts from my mother, whom they had been in touch with again that morning.

Jane approached me smiling, asking for a short interview and a new picture for the next issue of the magazine. Her smile spoke of her conviction that she was the kind of person who does you a favour for which you should be grateful. I still wonder, even now, what would have happened if I had refused to answer her questions. Would Yannis have stopped writing to me?

I agreed, and Jane's smile showed me that she had not expected me to refuse. I asked the supervisor to let me off for half an hour, and I followed them, leaving my apron on a chair in the kitchen.

Jane walked beside me to the Cinémathèque, where Kevin stopped in front of the big-windowed wall. The sun was reflected in the glass, casting a yellow glow all over de Maisonneuve. He told us he'd like to take some pictures here, adding that we did not need to set up any complicated background, as Yannis had liked me for my naturalness. I asked Jane if this picture was for the Canadian soldier in Afghanistan, but she ended the discussion briefly: "Don't listen to him! The picture is for everybody."

So Kevin took pictures of me in my bleached jeans and my close-fitting black T-shirt, which covered my belly button quite decently, as I have never been fond of exposing this part of my body. I was wearing my hair down, except for a few locks I'd clipped back near my forehead. My hands were in my pockets. I looked like any other girl in the street. Once the photography session was over, what remained was easy, as Jane had not come for the story of my whole life, just for a tiny part of it. I did not yet have the status of a star, and the space the magazine granted me was just a short column. The person who mattered in this story was Yannis, not me.

Jane wrote a few notes about my biography and my hobbies on her pad. I had always despised interviews in which celebrities unveiled their simplest pleasures to please their fans: a salad, a ride into the forest, an orange pullover, their dog, their car. How could people be so silly? What meaning does a daily routine have for a celebrity's career, and what is the connection between private pleasures and the public image?

When you're the one being interviewed, though, your view changes completely. I was suddenly aware how pleasant it was to have my life taken seriously and to think that people would be interested in my likes and dislikes. Routine can be interesting. Even if one person's habits, down to the smallest detail, are just like another's, they are all still unique and incomparable in the universal cycle of life. The alchemy which takes place in our mind when we are performing the very same acts of eating or making love remains an exclusive and indescribable process for each of us.

Under the pressure of Jane's questions, I discovered another being in me, someone eager to make herself known, to be revealed. What did I love the most in the world? Whatever could Jane possibly mean by this? For me it was not an easy question. On the contrary, it was charged with deep meaning. Do human beings ever understand what they do for pleasure or by force of habit? How much of it is just mimicry imposed by the herd? Which are our real joys? Do we ever know what we deeply love?

What should I have said? Should I have talked about my favourite authors? *Maclear's* was not a literary magazine, and my thesis on Postcolonial literature would have been too heavy for that readership. Names such as Salman Rushdie, Hanif Kureishi and Zadie Smith would mean something in a literary circle, but how could I summarize what *The Buddha of Suburbia*, for example, meant to the so-

cial paradigm in the late twentieth century? Should I have
spoken about what scholars were calling hyphenated iden-
tities? I could consider myself an expert in this field, and
I would have enjoyed talking about it. Jane came to my
rescue:

"What colour do you like?"

This was a more difficult question for me. I had never
questioned myself about my favourite colour. Who asks
themselves about their favorite colour, anyway? Was it red,
thanks to its gaudy strength of attraction and evocation? I
always envied women wearing red, which seemed to me an
act of courage. As for me, the only red thing I owned was
a wool scarf that I did not often wear, as I had nothing to
go with it.

White? Not sure. The only white thing I owned was
a skirt. Black? Maybe; my T-shirt was black, but what did
this mean? In a few seconds, I reviewed my whole wardrobe, my shoes and even the stones in my rings. Impossible
to make up my mind! This really was too hard a question to answer right away. What saved me was a passerby
waiting next to the red light, a young woman wearing an
emerald-green skirt. Her sandals, with flat soles, made her
look so light-hearted and carefree, that I said without any
hesitation:

"Green. I like green."

I wanted to add some details to this choice, as I imagined that if people were interested in my preferences, they
would also be interested in my reasons. But Jane rapidly
passed to the next question.

"Do you have any special meals or a place where you
go to eat?"

It was getting more and more complicated. Meals and
favourite restaurants? My brain became empty right away.
It had never occurred to me to rank the food I wolfed down
every day. Meals should definitely provoke in celebrities

such intense pleasure that they need to qualify and measure their food in a very special way. What did I like to eat? When did a meal give me so much pleasure as to darken my mind like a prolonged orgasm? I tried hard to think of a time in the past few days that had been as exciting as that, but all I could find were my mother's soups and macaroni, which I loved without making any big deal about it.

Meat, vegetables, dairy products, cakes, beverages? Canada's Food Guide unrolled quickly in my mind, for my mother had put the latest version up on the fridge, the one that increased fruit and vegetable portions yet again. It did no good, though; people were in love with meat and sweets. Maybe the problem was that portion sizes were not clearly enough explained. Was a glass of juice equal to a few apples or a basket of strawberries? A portion of apples could not be identical to one of orange juice or blueberries, could it?

Seeing me so disoriented, Jane helped me again. "Italian food, or maybe Chinese?"

So that's how it is. Celebrities' gastronomic preferences are counted in Italian and Chinese meals. What else could I say other than that I liked a good slice of all-dressed pizza? It was even on the menu at Les Trois Brasseurs. As soon as I thought about it, I remembered the whole menu of our restaurant, which also included mushroom soup and smoked meat sandwiches. I asked Jane to note that I like smoked meat sandwiches.

As my imagination started to roll, I told her I sometimes went to Schwartz's on St. Lawrence, to eat real smoked meat with pickles. I could see this moved me up a notch in Jane's eyes, as she also knew that small restaurant whose fame was bigger than the quality of its sandwiches. My God, what was the difference between the smoked meat sold under that name and that available in many other places? My mother could not tell the difference either, even though she came from the same country as Schwartz. But going to Schwartz's was more than eating smoked meat. For this question therefore, the right answer was that I liked smoked meat at Schwartz's.

Afterwards, Jane asked me how I would characterize myself in two words. I have no idea, Jane. Is it possible for two words to summarize somebody's personality and their life since childhood, including all the remorse, excesses of confidence, and complexes of all kinds?

Jane was not at all disposed to speculate on the matter; she was totally sure of what modern media could do. She offered me a short list from which I could choose what fitted me the best: "intelligent," "hard-working," "persevering," "realistic," "optimistic," "kind," "polite." I loved that list right away, with its positive view of human life. Is there anyone who would prefer instead to describe themselves as "stupid," "jealous," "lazy," or "pessimistic"?

Without thinking, I chose "intelligent" and "hard-working." Was this me? Not really, but who is a purist? Nevertheless, I felt guilty about my choices. For justice to be done, I told Jane I smoke a lot. Saying this during an anti-smoking campaign made me feel better, and so I figure I could have added "courageous" to Jane's list as well.

After only three questions, I felt the excitement of risky things. Here I was, faced with the secret machinery of public life, and human beings take pleasure in rebuilding their own identity. So I was disappointed when Jane had no other questions for me. She had me pegged as a smart and hard-working woman who loves the colour green and smoked meat sandwiches at Schwartz's.

She abandoned me with the same smile that showed me how grateful I should have been to her. Kevin was waiting nearby, smoking a cigarette. They went down to the métro station, and I waited a little while before going back to the restaurant, just enough time to smoke a cigarette.

When I entered the kitchen to put on my apron, nobody noticed my return since there was a huge number of rush hour customers, but by evening three men had asked me if I was the woman in the picture.

I guess this is the time I should tell you about Henry and Manuel, the two men in my life before Yannis.

I met Henry at a birthday party for Lina, a Chinese classmate. He was Chinese too. My relationship with him came just in time, as my mother was very worried about my solitude and asceticism, but whose fault was that, having me put in a school for girls, and Catholic to boot? I would have had more chance of becoming a lesbian, anyway, which was the reputation some of my classmates had.

Outside the grey school wall, people had all kinds of sexual fantasies about us, as we were wearing those kilts, with our knees naked. The girls contributed to those fantasies themselves, because as soon as they went through the big iron gates at the end of the school day, they shortened their skirts by rolling them up at the waist. We were very aware of the reputation a girl's school could have in the collective mentality.

I was Henry's friend for two years, but it was only towards the end of high school that we slept together. It was just a child's game, a mixture of timidity and shame. Henry represents the kind of experience that means nothing to a woman.

People imagine that the first time a woman makes love, it means a lot to her, as this is the point of no return, the moment of an irreversible conversion. A woman will never be the same again, for better or for worse. Which may be true. We usually associate the revelation of our own body to the small tear between our legs and to the smarting pain that comes with it, which is more of a surprise than it is painful. In my case, it was just the shame, religious shame in the face of sin, and that, too, was my parents' fault for having chosen Villa Maria.

Unfortunately, what my memory selected afterwards was just the smell of Henry's basement on an autumn afternoon while his parents were at work. He had set out a beach towel and a small cushion printed with big red chrysanthemums on the sofa, just for the occasion. Despite the warmth outside, inside it was chilly, and the air smelled slightly damp. The room was almost empty, as his family had installed neither a home cinema nor ping-pong nor a billiard table, as was the custom inside Canadian houses. I thought maybe his father was keeping the room for his yoga exercises. The window was covered by a double curtain that stopped the light filtering inside. To illuminate the room, Henry turned on a small lamp with a blue paper lampshade.

Henry came from a Chinese family from Hong Kong that had sought refuge in Canada when Hong Kong was transferred to China. The family was wealthy, and in their new country they had continued doing what Chinese people do best: trade. Their house had a motley mixture of expensive objects and cheap knick-knacks, and the air smelled of sandalwood, hotpot and jasmine tea. Colourful rugs spoke to the custom of removing shoes at the entrance and might have invited guests to feel a certain intimacy.

In my case, it was humility. Once I was barefoot, I did not know where to place my shoes, next to his mother's slippers or further on, under the wooden shelf where men and women's shoes were together, one on top of the other. Despite the atmosphere of tidiness and elegance in each room, the presence of certain objects revealed the kind of isolation that comes to a family whose guests all tend to share their own origins. I would not have known how and in what circumstances to use the thermos placed on a small table in the living room, which was surely filled with hot water.

Henry's father ran a secondhand furniture shop on Jean Talon West. Once I accompanied Henry there, as his father had asked him to go in for half an hour. He never introduced me to his father, just as I had never introduced Henry to my mother, even after two years of friendship. While Henry spoke to his father in the back office, I wandered through the store like any other customer.

The furniture was displayed on two levels in the big hall of an ancient factory, which had been turned into small shops. His father had set up cozy exhibits, like those in IKEA, to show the clients how to fit all those mismatched pieces together. As the chairs, tables, beds and dressers came from different houses, it needed a special adroitness to set them up. To improve the look of this bric-a-brac, he had included a few odd objects which were not for sale: bronze statues of Buddha, Chinese pottery, and pretty tea sets. People had to buy the all-included display.

That day I had to wait quite a long time, as Henry was working on the computer, assisted by his father, who stood behind him. They were occasionally interrupted by his father's associate, a Turkish guy. I sat in turn on frayed sofas and in armchairs covered in tapestry. Some pieces were real antiques that would have been better displayed in a museum. Even with my little knowledge of business, I thought the prices were high for this kind of furniture.

Henry said everything could be negotiated, but nobody ever succeeded in beating his father down. One way or another, he would charge the client for delivery or he would make them buy more in order to round up the amount of money. His father was a small man, skinny and almost ugly. His mother, of whom I have only seen a picture, was extremely beautiful. Henry looked like his mother.

Right from the start, our friendship was an adventure without a future. I don't know why this idea was set in both our minds the first day we met; we both felt like we were just Lina's friends. Things looked simple to us until Henry started to change. He suddenly grew up, and his voice became strong and sharp enough to break glass. When he laughed, he made such a noise that people turned to look at us. He let his hair grow long and put it up on top of his head in a samurai-like knot. Knowing something of the history of Hong Kong and the Japanese invasion, I had no doubt that his father was unhappy about that.

He was often asked to go and help his father in the shop, as part of secret preparations for the Turk's dismissal. Henry obeyed his father without enthusiasm, but his father paid him honestly. This was the best way to keep him interested, for Henry was quite stingy. The contact with his father's business was part of what changed him. By the end of the second year of our relationship, he was touching me more and more often, and when he proposed that we make love together I agreed right away. What I remember even to this day was my fear that his father would come home while we were still in the basement.

Our first love meeting took place without any preamble, and Henry remained silent throughout. Next time, things followed the same pattern. We went slowly down into the basement, as if this would convince us of the seriousness of our act, undressed discreetly, each of us in the opposite corner, and then afterwards, we parted without a big farewell.

I imagined that what was spoiling Henry's pleasure was the same fear as mine, that his father would return while we were still naked. I knew Henry would have shielded me if that had happened, but I also knew he would have been mortally embarrassed. I saw Henry as an honest and brave young man, but at the same time I guessed his childish weakness and suspected the terrible gulf that our relationship would have opened up between him and his parents.

Each time I went home, I was grateful to him for his silence and decency. Neither of us knew what to say in such a situation. What embarrassed us most was our shame at trying to act like adults.

I was in my first semester at Marianopolis College when Henry invited me to his place one afternoon, as usual. He had just got back from the store, which should have reassured me his father would not be around. For the first time, though, I refused to go. I was tired and overwhelmed by the changes that had recently taken place in my life. Big changes were rare in my experience, and I had always had a long period when I could get used to the idea of my father's departure, my mother's remarriage, and my enrolment at Villa Maria.

What I was having trouble with now was the switch from French school to English college, new classmates, and new teachers. I took refuge every day in my mother's cosy apartment, and the day Henry called I had no intention of leaving the house. It was a natural feeling of protectiveness, and he should have understood. But he did not. He stopped calling me and I never made any attempt to contact him. I accepted that my initial intuition had been right, and the relationship had no future. And I realized that associating my anti-social mother with a Chinese businessman from Hong Kong who ran a second-hand furniture store on Jean Talon would have been really awkward.

So I was alone again, and I did not dislike it. Unlike my mother, I was not at all worried at being on my own. I have never told her what happened with Henry, but she knew. She knew right away, when I got home after having been down in the basement with Henry that first time, and she passed over the occasion in silence, just as Henry had. I spent my Cégep years in the company of girls of many different origins and languages. I was particularly close to the Chinese girls, who reminded me of my relationship with Henry, whom I had not met since that phone call. I did happen to see him a couple of times in the street, but I didn't call out to him.

Once I started at university I went to work, which my mother has never accepted. Why did I have to work, she did not stop wondering, as my father paid my tuition fees and she took care of room and board? What kind of cruel system was this that forces young people to spend the best years of their lives deadening their minds? She would never get used to the North American way of life. In her mind, at this age young people should spend their time reading or just relaxing, letting their mind work instead. Traveling a little bit on their own, wandering here and there, visiting people or family.

Instead of acquiring wisdom, North America pushed them to deaden their minds, just to gain experience. How awful these words were: North American experience. And what kind of experience was it, anyway? On your feet eight hours a day for a pittance that soon vanished on a few jars of cosmetics, nylon thongs, and a couple of lunches at McDonald's? Why were people's standards so low? They naively trusted the propaganda of a consumer society that turned them into slaves in a cycle empty of value and personality.

My father agreed with me, and not just because my working reduced the amount he had to pay for my schooling. He was much more at ease with North American values than my mother, and he called her old-fashioned and a Communist.

Manuel came into my life in big, bold steps. He was a supervisor at the box company where I had been hired thanks to one of my classmates, who had worked there for about two months. It was because of Manuel that I stayed there for more than a year. The routine of working at the conveyer belt was a killer. I had to stand motionless for eight hours and stick silk fabric inside paper or plastic boxes. That was the task I was assigned at the beginning, and it never changed.

The company produced containers, from small boxes for jewels to money or gold ingot boxes. For larger orders from banks and other corporate clients, they had to hire extra staff. During the normal season, there was a team of about 30 people, most of them Asians and Latinos.

It was like an ancient slave galley and, once aboard, you never left. There were some old women who had been working there for more than 20 years and who spoke neither of the two official languages. When the supervisors wanted to teach them new things to do, they had to show the woman what to do. If they had to correct the women, they just said, No good! At lunchtime, these women clustered together in a small corner to speak their own language and eat their fish and rice with old wooden chopsticks. Nobody dared to stop them bringing in such stinky meals, so all of us had to eat our lunch in a room smelling of microwaved fish.

When they had to design new kinds of boxes, the two bosses made an appeal for the Chinese men's services. Together, they drew and built up the new models in paper, which were cast afterwards in plastic molds. For the inside and outside cover, a special team was needed, and Manuel was often asked to help. Most of the work was done by hand because machines were not able to fix the delicate satin pleats.

Each time I ended up lining a box in red silk, I asked myself where it was going to, to whom, and for what necklace or ring. What man was going to offer a precious gift in this box, and to what woman? I was sure this kind of nonsense was on the Asian women's minds, too. They must have made up their own fantasies that one could no longer read on their exhausted faces.

At the end of the day, their features were almost shapeless, their eyes haggard, their slightly open lips hanging, and their backs bent, scarcely able to support their heads, which were crowned with short, disheveled curls. Those women were a gloomy sight every day, worse even than the monotony of the work.

I used to terrify myself, trying to imagine what their lives were like outside the workshop, thinking about their very small portion of human happiness. After work, I imagined, they would head home promptly to prepare supper, and they would go to bed early so they would be able to punch in on time next morning. And their lives would continue like that, day after day, in this huge, grey, mournful space with its filthy glass walls, where they would stand next to these greasy machines and breathe in air that smelled of glue.

My mother's life was not at all like those of the women who were working here, and she fought to keep me away from these vivid examples of human failure. She knew better than I how tiredness destroys a person's hopes and dreams.

I would soon have left the company if it hadn't been for Manuel. His kindness, and later on his passion for me, made me put up with the place. After just a few weeks, I was no longer judging the women I worked with, for I myself had I started to look like them: my mouth remained half-open. I got used to their tiny share of happiness as, yes, humans can build their well-being on small things. A day off, for example, when the company had few orders, was a source of pleasure. The employees returned home earlier than usual and for the rest of the day they sat on their balcony watching children playing around the public pool.

Manuel was Spanish, and he had arrived in Canada more than 20 years before. He held a Master's degree in psychology from the University of Madrid, but as an immigrant he had been unable to find a job in his field. He therefore temporarily entered the factory and never left because, thanks to his education, he was named supervisor of a team of 30 people.

His pay was not much higher than that of the workers; I think that what kept him there was his title rather than the work. His job was ten times more exhausting than that of his employees. As they only spoke their mother tongue, he had to show them what to do and how to do it for every new project with his own hands. He also had to keep watching them for a few days afterwards to reduce the amount of material wasted.

Manuel was my elder by about 21 years. He was divorced, but his wife lived in the same building with their ten-year-old son. When I lived with Manuel, we often came across each other in the stairwell or the entrance hall. Their separation was rather like a marriage lived on different floors, and my arrival upset their relationship. She finally realized that she no longer had exclusivity with this man, and the idea that another woman held him in her arms made her crazy with jealousy.

Manuel was experiencing the same kind of ambivalence. The effect our love had on his wife made him wonder if he had been right to divorce her. He would make love with her when I was away and whenever I said anything about this, he would laugh in such a way that I understood I did not have the right to reproach him. He gave this right to his ex-wife only, though he did his best not to bump into her too often in the building.

His son had a habit of coming to us almost every day to eat or ask for money. Even during Manuel's absence, the kid would dash into the apartment without ringing, make himself at home on the sofa in front of the TV, and ask me for ice cream. A little later, his mother would come looking for him, and she would also come into my apartment to check up on the state of things. Most of Manuel's furniture came from their ménage, and as she still felt like its real owner, she glared at me for using it.

After a while, I refused to let the boy in. Each time he rang the bell, I stood on the doorstep, holding an ice cream in one hand and a couple of loonies in the other, and then I locked the door. Probably his wife told Manuel off about this, but he did not have the energy to make me change my mind. I told him to go and see his family in their own apartment, which, in a way, was an invitation to go and see his wife and do whatever he liked. Strangely, I was not jealous at all.

I know I was not a good housekeeper. I did not know how to cook, and I often forgot to do the laundry and clean. When Manuel dared occasionally to show me some small displeasure, I did not feel guilty nor did I try to get him to forgive me. My ineptitude did not affect our relationship, because Manuel remained extremely polite and gentle. At the time, I considered his attitude as proof of his love. I now know he took me for a spoiled child, and he thought it unworthy for a man to insist I behave in a mature way.

He just wanted to keep me. The age difference excited him erotically. I am sure about this, even though I have not had any other boyfriends since. A woman matures sexually even when she does not make love. Thinking about my relationship with Manuel today, I find it quite creepy in many ways. It's amazing how the desire for sexual pleasure can get us to accept such inauspicious circumstances. We are ready to track down what is wrong with other people's relationships, but never with our own.

At the time, despite his wife glaring at me, and his

boy's mischief, I was happy. Every day, I waited impatiently for nightfall to make love. I was insatiable, especially when I compared Manuel to Henry, who had been so shy and clumsy. Manuel was a little plump, sweet to caress, tender. His sex, when erect, seemed to have a life of its own. His rigid organ awoke in Manuel a roughness that he tried to hide so as not to frighten me. Since our first contact, he understood my lack of experience and he tried not to play the teacher with me, while he enjoyed the pleasure that only sex with a young woman can provoke in an older man.

To calm my fears, he just had to hug me, envelop me in his muscular arms, kiss my lips, caress my hair, and touch my ear when he came. Afterwards, he took care not to fall asleep immediately, but to talk a little nonsense. His consideration for me, and his curiosity about my trivial stories, reduced the discomfort that follows sex. Manuel knew how embarrassing it is for a woman when her partner starts snoring beside her.

The lack of illusion about our relationship put some distance between us right from the beginning. The fact that neither Manuel nor I ever considered having a baby and thus perpetuating our mixed genes made our relationship a relaxing Sunday affair. And this feeling both increased our passion and limited our love.

Manuel took charge of almost everything. I made only a tiny contribution to upkeep and finances. My life with him was extremely convenient. His passion helped me overcome the cosmic fatigue caused by the job. I wondered where he got the energy to keep going after ten hours running back and forth in the maze of machines. Through exercise, an individual becomes less and less complex. The rhythm of our activities gradually makes us unsophisticated, and this minimalism is transferred to our desires. The less we do, the less we want.

Manuel comforted me in my revolt against the monotony of the work. That's what happens, he said, when a person is still holding on to the 1,000 possibilities of their terrestrial journey. Why 1,000? How did he figure that was the number of chances a person has of becoming some-body else? He did not know, but 1,000 is a nice, round number. Imagine that you could live in 999 other places and be 999 other people.

Me, I have chosen to be the daughter of a divorced family, who comes from Dracula's country, an ordinary student and seasonal worker in a box factory. How can I know what the other 999 alternatives might be?

While he was preparing the spaghetti sauce for dinner, maybe Manuel wondered about the other 999 alternatives for his own life. The diligence he put into domestic chores must have had something to do with the fact that he did not know how to solve that mystery. But he did not talk too much about this: the difference between a young per-son and an adult is that the former keeps on questioning himself and others as well. Adolescents are not far from the age where, like children, they ask big people to resolve their anxieties. Any answer, even when it is wrong, reas-sures them. Instead of trying to fool me, Manuel was such an honest man that he acknowledged his ignorance of the best solution for the best possible life. He told me sincerely: "I do not know."

I eventually realized that I did not have to make things more difficult that they already were. Manuel had no other vocation besides making love to me and preparing a good dinner. He was not stupid, but he wisely tried to reduce the sadness of his failure. And who decided his life was a failure? He had his own life, and everything was going well. I was there, and he was very happy, for he had never foreseen this possibility in his life. Here you are, proof that we can trust our destiny.

I often went shopping with Manuel, if only to keep him company among shelves overflowing with plastic bags, boxes and packets. Food was kept far from the sense of smell and the sense of touch: it was nothing more than images printed on paper boxes.

I was used to my mother's pace, as she spent a lot of time reading labels and patiently going through the shelves searching for exotic products. Manuel had no time for this: he always went to the same places and bought what he already knew. I did not agree with his choice of groceries, but I did not get involved. Eating so much pizza and spaghetti would undoubtedly have consequences one day, but would I live with Manuel long enough to be worried about his health?

We went to work together, but I often came back alone, because I did not want to work overtime. Manuel did not stay because he wanted to but because he had to. I took the bus and returned home quickly to sleep.

Summer passed almost unremarked with this routine that was enlivened only by sex. We had no other pleasure or leisure except under the sheets. We ate and watched TV for a while, skipping from one channel to another, undecided between talk shows and American movies. Manuel's apartment was ugly and almost empty. He had neither the time nor the energy to take care of it.

I got ready to go to bed first, as showers took me a long time. Afterwards, I went straight into the bedroom and waited for Manuel, who washed himself in no time. While I was waiting for him, I did not even pretend to read a magazine or a book: when he entered the room, he was surprised that I was watching the door. He sat on the bed, and his eyes warned me of his intentions. I welcomed him all naked.

Manuel lay at my side and started caressing me while

looking up and down my body. One of his hands passed under my nape, as if he wanted to hold me in his arms, while his other hand gently wandered between my neck and my belly. A little later, he got to my sex, after having kissed my lips for a long time: the slight pressure of his fingers made me understand that I had to spread my legs. I burned with impatience for him to penetrate me, as I was ashamed of how wet I was. Manuel took his time, for at his age an erection is not that fast. I could have helped him, caressed and encouraged him, but at that time I did not know that. I learned that later, from a book.

Sex with me was always in the same position, as Manuel was ashamed to ask me for more involvement. As for me, what he did to me was utterly fulfilling. I burned with excitement at every touch, especially when Manuel's hand went under my buttocks to hold me up, to accommodate his sex. In all this, I had nothing to do, as Manuel was my guide and my master, and I wisely obeyed him.

This state could not continue for long. I knew that Manuel would slow down, and that that would make me gloomy and, in the long run, scornful. I would not accept any other kind of treatment or longer breaks. I felt that this time was going to come, which would hurt Manuel and make me unhappy. I left him before that moment arrived.

My mother had been so sad seeing me living with a man who was almost her own age. But she always excelled in not involving herself in my business. She was more embarrassed than I by the affair and avoided the subject. I did not go and see her often and when I did, we just talked about my studies. Sometimes I gave her books to read and then visited her on the pretext of taking them back.

After a while, though, she no longer worried about my relationship. She had already guessed it wouldn't last much longer. My mother was up to date with my interior upheavals. At the time when I started to question my relationship with Manuel, she asked why didn't I move into her flat as she had lived alone for more than half a year. I accepted and left Manuel, who allowed me to leave with no further questions. He suffered, I saw that clearly, but he knew this would happen sooner or later. He also wanted to avoid an embarrassing situation that could hurt a man's pride. The saddest thing was that he was going to fall under his wife's thumb and his son's tyrannical presence again. He could not stand it anymore.

Soon after, he moved to an unknown address. I went once to look for him and to make love, but he was no longer there. I knocked at his wife's door to ask for his address, even though I knew her reaction beforehand. She slammed the door in my face.

The message from Corporal Yannis Alexandridis came one Saturday morning. It was in the middle of my junk mail, and I almost deleted it, as his address *Yannis75@hotmail.com* didn't tell me anything. I don't usually open messages from unknown senders. However, the subject was "Hello from Kandahar," which is why I didn't delete it. I still hesitated for a while, but in the end I decided to open it.

Hi Irina,

I am sending you greetings from Kandahar. I think you already know who I am. I've dared to write a few words to you, and I'm afraid you will think I just want to flirt. What girl wouldn't? Here, where I am, we are less able to judge the appropriateness of certain things. We live with our regrets about not having dared to do everything we wish to. And after having seen your picture, I'm dying to talk to you. I want to know if your mortarboard was real, if the picture was taken the day you graduated, many other questions.

I also wonder if you are angry with me because the magazine published my letter about you. I have to acknowledge that it has brought me a certain celebrity status over here, though that isn't why I sent it. The captain has not stopped making fun of me, and the lads have made me a mortarboard on which they pinned the regimental badge. They told me that as long as I admire women holding diplomas, I should have one myself. In fact I do have one, but not in literature. They pinned my letter to Maclear's up next to your cover picture, and everyone complains to me for having talked about their little actions at the checkpoint instead of talking about their braveries. They told me what should I write in my next letter to you, and to be sure I'm not wrong about the places where we pushed back the Taliban, they wrote all those strange village names on a piece of paper.

I threw away their notes because there won't be a second letter to Maclear's. I am happy they sent me your address on the understanding that it was your mother who gave it to them. Thank your mom on my behalf. I will stop here, and if you do not want to answer me, I will understand. Yannis

I answered him right away and then regretted it five minutes later. That's the way it is with email; we press the send button before thinking about it.

Here is my note, replying to his.

Re: Hello from Kandahar.
Hi Yannis,
The mortarboard is not mine, and the picture was not taken at my graduation. I am still at school. As you see, somebody is always making fun of us.

Irina

I stayed in front of the computer for more than an hour, as if Yannis were waiting for my message on the other end. What time was it in Kandahar? I waited for a while, surfing the Internet, looking for information on Zadie Smith's last novel. It was difficult to find literary references to her among thousands of articles on her life and tastes, published in women's magazines where she had frequently appeared since the publication of her first novel, *White Teeth*.

I got no reply that day.

The next day, Yannis's message was in my inbox, after a long list of messages about penis enlargements and prices for Viagra.

The message was called Mortarboard.

Hello, Irina,

If the mortarboard is not true, then is what is written in the latest issue of Maclear's true?
Y

Re: Mortarboard
Yes, everything is true, but the list of true things about me is very long. I don't know if you have enough time.
I

Time
At this very moment, I have enough time. I know nothing about tomorrow.
Y

Re: Time
You didn't answer me. It was not a matter of time but of interest.

I
Interest
Is your list that long?
Y

I did not reply to this note. Not immediately. Suddenly, this game exhausted me. Things were shifting, and I knew it was because of me. Statistically, women are the biggest experts in ruining their friendships through email. All my female friends had lived similar stories of losing good friends because of messages coming and going too fast. I shouldn't have written to him. Not like that. I shut myself up for two days. Yannis's next letter arrived on Tuesday, around 6 p.m.

Hello again
Irina,
I was up North for a while. However, this is not the reason I did not write to you. Is everything all right? Could we start again?
Y

Re: Hello again
Tell me about you. Let's forget about the list. What the magazine has written about me is enough for the moment. Now it's your turn.
I

From his next letter, I learned that Yannis was of Greek origin. In fact, his last name had not left me in any doubt about that, and the fact that he originated in Greece was not a happy discovery. My mother's people had been neighbours of Yannis's people for a very long time, and history had taught us that his people had caused mine a lot of trouble.

In the 17th century, the Turks, who were suzerains of the Romanian territories, put the Phanariots on the throne of Wallachia, scum gathered in the worst part of Istanbul, Phanar. These new masters exploited the most wretched people in the country, the peasantry, over a period of more than a hundred years that had no precedent in Romanian history. Clerics were selected from among the Greek clergy, and local priests and monks were willing to be ruined by such erudite men, mistakenly associating them with the noble tradition of Plato and Aristotle. Greek traders took over the marketplace, cheating on weight and not giving change back to illiterate buyers.

In short, the Greeks had left such a bad legacy that there's a Romanian saying, *Beware of Greeks even if they bear gifts.* Let me acknowledge the classical source of this old proverb, as it draws its wisdom from the story of Ulysses and the Trojan Horse. Apparently, in ancient times, the Greeks were not that bad, as the Trojans only said: *Beware of Greeks when they bear gifts.*

Here is why my relationship with Yannis started out on the wrong foot. He was Greek, and therefore I figured he must be a scoundrel. Bored with his life in Kandahar, he was accosting girls on the Internet. If he had had different origins, I might have seen him differently. A therapist from Vancouver just published a book on how to survive a date with a person from another ethnic group: in other words, how to overcome sexual culture shock. Dating someone with a background other than your own is something that people in Canada have to learn.

The first thing to know is never to be jealous of the time that the ethnic partner spends with his family. On the other hand, the ethnic partner should not be worried if the Canadian refuses to marry him. The Canadian does not have to be stuck with only one minority group, like Asians or Africans: from time to time, they have to try some other races.

If a Canadian woman makes love with an ethnic guy, she should not be outraged by the fact that he definitively refuses to perform cunnilingus on her: what prevents him from doing so is not necessarily his fear of vagina dentata, but the idea of serving a woman.

This therapist unfortunately does not propose any solution for white Europeans. In Canada, the word ethnic conjures up spicy meals, dark skin, covered heads, red marks on the forehead, orange turbans, and henna-dyed beards. So what happens with Polish people who still have some problems to sort out with Russians, Czechs with Germans, Bulgarians with Turks, Serbs with Albanians, and Romanians with Greeks? Obviously, we have to wait for another book to give us advice on dealing with ethnics from Europe.

Yannis's letter was not long: in it, he told me that his parents came to Canada shortly before he was born, when his sister was two years old. His mother, who was a very religious woman, chose a name for him related to Jesus. Not daring to call him Christos, she gave him the Baptizer's name, Yannis. He grew up in Montreal, where his mother still lives when she is not back in Greece. After his father's death from cancer, she started spending a lot of time in her native country. Yannis's sister became a biology teacher and recently moved to the United States.

His family situation was clearly not very happy. What happened to the house when his mother was overseas? And where did he live when he was home on leave?

I spent a long time wondering if I should ask him this question. I was afraid he would take my feminine curiosity about domestic details badly. So I decided not to ask that question, and instead asked what he was doing in Afghanistan. This soon looked like an even worse idea.

His reply came right away.

Re: Question
What we do is fine drivers who park their cars badly. Sometimes we even stop Taliban who cross the street on a red light.
Y

As a soldier, Yannis was definitively heir to Achilles who, of all the warriors besieging the city of Troy, was the one most likely to lose his temper. Or maybe war sharpens the susceptibility in any combatant's soul. The worst is when civilians doubt the services that an army carries out on behalf of their country. I did not know how to answer this letter: if I had hurt him, I did not care too much about it. A soldier, especially a Greek soldier, at my door was difficult for me to bear.

Half an hour later, I opened another message from Yannis, also in response to mine:

Re: Question
Irina,
I apologize for what I said. Despite the corpses that return home almost every day, in a way people imagine we're here on a kind of holiday. They know soldiers die in Afghanistan, but not everyone steps on a mine, and generally the army is too well equipped – Internet, food, booze – for people to feel sorry for us. The question is: Do you really want to talk about what I am doing here? You will be sorry because what I am going to tell you is surely not what you want to hear. Your Afghanistan is a mirage, mine is a nightmare.

For example, someone said Kandahar , where I am posted, was once an earthly paradise. The vineyards and orchards of peach trees, fig trees and mulberry tree were famous all around the world. Images of Kandahar's pomegranates embellished ancient Persian manuscripts. Before the war, Afghan trucks full of fruits traveled to Calcutta. Soviets destroyed the irrigation system and cut down the trees, as mujahedeen fighters hid amongst them. All that is left are the ruins of ancient orchards. Even today, these places are the most mined lands in the world. Local peasants who venture over there return blinded or with their legs blown off. And every new field cleared of mines is used for poppy culture. But as long as this kind of agriculture is so fruitful for the anemic local economy, even women are allowed to go and work in the fields.

I feel a little bit dizzy because of the high air pressure. The wind carries the dust everywhere, out of rocks, trellis walls, and muddy roads. The air is always dry and to filter it you need a nose as strong as a pump. We are getting used to breathing through this reddish flour, which floats in the air from dawn until sunset.

I have to stop. I'm leaving and hope to be back by evening.
Y

I waited a day for his letter, but it did not come. What did happen, though, was that I had a phone call from Henry. He had read the article about me when it was first published in *Maclear's*, but it was not until the news was taken up again by the big newspapers that he became eager to see me again. Henry was in his third year of an undergraduate electrical engineering course at McGill University. His parents had returned to Hong Kong. After a period of fear and indecision, they decided that the Chinese Communist domination of Hong Kong was not that bad, as long as it permitted certain outlets. The older generation of refugees in Canada felt secure enough to go back and reopen their businesses as long as Chinese citizens from the mainland were kept at the border, needing a visa to enter Hong Kong.

Henry did not want to stay in Canada either. His parents' experience had shown him that Chinese people did not succeed that well in this freezing country and also that Canadians' business ventures in China ended in bankruptcy. There was a deep incompatibility between these two nations when it came to the language of money. Henry, advised or forced by his father, was going to return to a land where he would master a specific and ancestral code of trade. He was living in a tiny apartment on campus and had a part-time job with his father's former partner, the Turk, who was now running the second-hand furniture store on Jean Talon.

It was strange to discover that in a country that changes its habits at an amazing speed, some people were still faithful to their trades. At present, the Turk was reigning over the dusty furniture empire. The only changes he had made, Henry told me, were the removal of the Buddhas, which he had replaced with Persian rugs and Ottoman hookahs.

The next day, Yannis came up with another letter about Afghanistan:

I wish I could tell you more about the real Afghanistan, but at present, as before, this country is just fiction. As you must know, to describe fiction takes more fiction. This may be the reason for our constant failure. We are trying to get together alongside two pieces of fiction that work in very different ways.

People used to call Afghanistan 200 years ago a buffer country between the British Empire, which was
ruling India, and Tsarist Russia. And now? Which
are the countries between which Afghanistan is the
buffer? Iran and Pakistan on one side? The United
States and China on the other? Who can say? What
is obvious is that we cannot help them. They don't
want our help. Not in terms of our fiction. They want
to be backed up on their own terms: that we make
changes here and there, but nothing changes, that's
what they want. What kind of soldiers are we? And
what are we doing here? Don't hold your breath for
answers from me because I don't know. The saddest
thing is that nobody knows. That we are still here is,
probably, due to the shame of being so powerless.

This country could be thought of as being like Borat's
Kazakhstan. Any Western comedian can joke about
this country, without censure, saying that rape is a national hobby. We can attribute the cruellest intentions
to these people, the strangest sexual behavior, but we
will never know the truth about them. War is designed
in such a way that defeated people are never right.
What is good for us is not good for them, that's what a
good soldier ends up understanding.

I suspect the name of this country fills your heart with
wonder. For many of us, though, the thrill has gone.
And this gloomy feeling turns us away from the rightness and beauty of their cause, if any. We no longer
know anything about it because this country changes
its multiple faces so fast. What seems today a wise apa-
thy in the attitude of our real or imaginary adversaries
could instantly turn tomorrow into the cruelest tor-

ture. Within this mixture of hate, threat and loneliness you just need clear-sightedness to perceive the beauty of these places, the purity that spontaneously comes out of the filth. Behind its usual dryness and dull colours, one autumn morning the desert thrills your heart with a fresh and amazing face.

Right now, I can see my friend Rasul riding his donkey, stuffed hemp knapsacks dangling on either side of the animal, and I know that we will always aim next to the target, not at it. I know what he is trafficking in these bags but I have no authority to interfere. In their eyes you can read the accusation that we have destroyed their homeland. They think that, because of us, the magnificent cities of yesteryear get uglier from one day to the next, and their streets are nothing more than dangerous back alleys.

My computer time is up, I have to give up my place.

Y

Henry has asked me to go out with him to have a coffee or see a movie.

This kind of activity is for teenagers on a first date who don't know how to fill the hours before going to bed and making love. It amused me, but I suddenly realized on the phone that behind my amusement I was feeling contempt for my former lover. Why had he waited so long before inviting me for coffee? Did my unexpected celebrity status change his perception of me?

Henry said no, but I knew it did. Everyone tries hard to hang out with celebrities, for we are taught from childhood that successful people have their faces in the newspaper. Money is worth nothing compared to a small article in an insignificant magazine.

Henry's surfacing did not therefore stop my flow of questions on the war Yannis was waging in Afghanistan. I simply asked him if he agreed with it. His answer came very quickly, which made me think that he was hanging around the garrison waiting for a new mission.

Re: Soldier.

I no longer ask myself that. When you're a soldier, this question doesn't exist anymore. Being a soldier is an identity in itself, and the war is his identity, a transnational identity. At war, soldiers act in the same way, everywhere, at any time. The hardest thing is when he starts asking himself what you are asking me right now.

As for my own reasons for being here, the country always has stronger reasons than an individual. We get used to being right or wrong along with our country. And a soldier is always only on one side. That is the law. I am neither a criminal nor a hero, I am a soldier. A soldier is in turn a criminal and a hero, depending on many things. What matters is that since I face death every day, I understand how fast things can change in a man's life, and I greatly appreciate that this life still exists. I accept any change as long as I am still here.

Our conflict is bigger than weapons, if you understand me. We have nothing to defend here if not the entire West, everything we have created and maintained. This is nothing more than a matter of pride. We cannot go back before getting proof that we did something worthwhile here. And the longer we stay, the harder this is to bear, as change is not noticeable at all.

Don't listen to what people say on TV, as everyone is embarrassed to have sent us to such an old country where spirits are still ruling over people. These places are legendary because of centuries of crime and guerrilla warfare. Even obscurity has a secret life here, and we feel eyes spying on us from every corner and even from the branches of trees.

I know people say we are waging a war against barbarians, but the barbarians they talk about are simply afraid to long for things they are taught to despise. While staring at us, their eyes reflect hate and nostalgia at the same time. They don't forget that if nowadays the desert covers their country, this land once was Eden, filled with flourishing cities, golden bridges and towers, wooden-paved streets, and magnificent gardens. They are survivors of a legendary past that is as real as their ruined present.

As for their life, the majority of them are living in the Middle Ages, ruled by secret laws which teach them to distrust anything that comes from the outside world. They never trust things that don't fit their rules. They particularly doubt what comes through us, as they know it would never be possible for them to match our teachings with their way of life. The dust, the desert, the closeness to their animals make their existence look crude, but on the other hand their ability to survive is unequalled. I am jealous of their will to survive and I think that, well equipped and armed to the teeth as we are, we have nothing to envy. We don't inquire any more about the rightness or the morality of their acts. Once you get here, you learn how worthless all this moral crap is. The problem with war is that people forget the troops and the ideals that inspire each camp. Everything that has a concrete meaning for us turns into a symbolic message for them. And due to this sibylline thinking they see through us as you might see through a plastic bag. No words can ever reveal their secrets to us. We trust numbers and maps; they only trust their instinct. Their intuition is their own and it's their best weapon. Their human skin is just a thin layer that hardly hides their terrible ancient being, ready at any moment to come out. Sometimes, I think even deaf and blind people feel our presence. We are woven out of doubt; they are woven out of passion. They teach us that what makes the body suffer turns all the soul's troubles into insignificant nonsense.

The longer I stay here, the deeper the desert kills any nostalgia. We start distrusting our past and we avoid more and more taking refuge in the good times in our memories. The contact with them should cure us of nostalgia and uproot our soul's neurosis. We should learn how to start a new life, without useless desires.

Y

Do you think, like me, that horrors need few words to be spoken? Pain is impossible to bear even when you describe it. Compare the number of words we use describing nonsense.

This letter convinced me to refuse Henry. I no longer wanted to meet him again. I did not want to see anybody, as the Canadian soldier had caught me. I despised myself for the ease with which I let myself be trapped. I wanted to be his prey. Suddenly, I realized that Yannis was in danger from morning till night, and that every single one of his steps was unsafe. Damn the Phanariot regime in Romania. We are only responsible for our own deeds.

Yannis was fighting a war that his ancestors started under the rule of Alexander the Great. The Macedonian's brave soldiers were charmed by the promises made by the young King. They left Greece to stop the Persian threat and to kill Darius. After the Persian army was defeated and Darius stabbed by one of his own generals, Alexander changed the aim of his campaign: from that point, he was leading a war to punish the traitor and avenge Darius.

Once the Persian general had been killed, Alexander once again changed his target. From that point on, he wanted nothing more than to travel, to reach the Indus shore and then return to Greece from the other end of the world, for his teacher Aristotle had taught him that the Earth is round, not flat. His soldiers therefore became explorers. They reached Caucasus, the land of the terrible turbaned dwellers. Due to the cold weather, the dust and the continuous harassment of the guerilla warriors, however, they started doubting what they were doing in that Afghan valley. After years and years of war in the desert lands where Yannis was now fighting, the Greek army said no to Alexander's desire to move forward. Soldiers usually obey orders until the day they have had enough and take the outcome of the battle into their own hands.

Were there any souvenirs in Yannis's secret memory of this ancient participation in the first big conquest? If there were, then he might appreciate Alexander's reasons for invading other people's lands, which were much more decent than the new ones, which consisted of just a few oil wells and a gas pipeline.

What prompted him to enter the army? The pay? Money certainly plays an important role in men's decision to fight, as war has always been the most profitable career of all. I think, though, that for many, at least for Yannis, money was not the strongest argument. Men remain the biggest travelers in this world, spurred on by the taste for adventure. What are the dreams that haunt their souls?

I asked Yannis what he feared most.

Re: Fear
I fear their faith, as its first law is terror. For them, only blood exorcises evil, and that really scares me. I fear this religion that is no longer founded on rituals but on terror. Y

My message left instantly, as for the first time I realized I shared the same religion with Yannis, which we never question. The West is so preoccupied by the conflict with Muslim people that we have lost sight of what we represent.

His message came back right away, as if Yannis had guessed my doubts. I was so happy that he also understood that we kept on talking about everything else in the world just to avoid talking about ourselves. Our meeting through intermediaries was so embarrassing. The public voice that had thrown us into each other's arms imposed a certain chastity on us. We became what others expected of us, something other than ourselves.

Re: What about us?

Irina, you ask me weird questions, which prompt me to respond with what I suppose must be annoying answers. Would it be possible, one day, to speak about ourselves?

To answer you: when I was a small boy, my mother often took me to church. She was not a fanatical believer, just a practicing Christian as a result of tradition; many Orthodox people are for the same reasons. What astonished me at that time, as we had some mandatory religion classes in school, was the uniqueness of our God in our Orthodox religion. We did not share our love for God either with his son, poor Jesus, or with the Apostles who nevertheless did the toughest job among the unbelievers. We don't know how to be grateful to those who do the hard work and who died in unenviable ways.

Our religion gives priority to a profound divinity, far from our soul, which is severe, selfish, vengeful, and jealous. There are too many prohibitions and too little freedom. I understand now how Communism could arise in an Orthodox country, in Rasputin's mystical Russia. People were already used to a powerful and authoritarian divinity. The more restrictive and tyrannical he was with his own people, the more they loved him. Above anything else, our religion believes in repentance, in endless abstinence and in self-criticism. We are used to believing that happiness lies in asceticism, in complexes, in the fear of wishing. Everything can get in the way of our salvation: too much food, too many words, the wind, sights, clothes, books, trips, friends. Everything that could make our life nicer is a threat to our eternal being. The example of Jesus Christ who was punished without being guilty smashed any hope when I was a child. If he died in this unjust manner, then we have no chance of resurrection either. But what about people from other religions: Catholics, Jews, Muslims? Are they happier with their God than we are? Why does anyone ask people to make so many sacrifices? Why is it all about surrender?

Y

Yannis was a non-believer. Doubting God and his own

mission in the army must be awful in wartime. I hoped that
at least he had friends among the lads. This is why I asked
him to write about his comrades.

Before getting his message, which took two days to
come, I received a funny call. A publicity agency asked
me to pay them a visit, as they wanted me to play a part
in a commercial. What kind of commercial? This was the
problem: they had not yet decided if I was the appropriate
image for a new car, a soap, a shampoo, the new autumn
season at Reitman's or Simons, a new recipe for lasagna
with Emmenthal, the new bioactive yogurt, a washing machine, or a cold water detergent.

I felt overwhelmed by this demand, and I asked my
mother for advice. Should I accept this offer? She answered
serenely and with no hesitation: Why not? For her the reason was neither money nor celebrity status, but curiosity.
I certainly should go: shooting in the desert, climbing a
mountain in white running shoes, cooking in a new sauce-
pan – my mother was burning with curiosity for me to tell
her how it was. Hadn't I asked myself what would happen
afterwards? After what, Mom?

My mother was not so naive as not to understand that
behind the magical world there was a crew of cameraman,
wardrobe masters, and make-up people. Still! My mother
was seduced by the gargantuan lies that she wished with all
her heart to believe in.

Publicity standardizes beauty, and it is mostly addressed to a public of white people. The faces of the
women who smile at the camera on behalf of goods rang-
ing from beauty products to winter tires or stainless steel
pots all look like one another, like so many drops of water. They are identical especially in the joy that comes
of acquiring the product, whether skin moisturizer or

long-life batteries, a new hat or a new kind of Campbell's soup. Buying itself is the biggest delight, not the product.

My mother sent me to spy behind the scenes at the moment when the wizards of happiness start feeling the anxiety of falsity, the moment when they switch off the lights and the smile freezes. It was my job to shed some light on this transition – and on this heartless drama.

So here you are, a woman coming out of a sky blue lake with a foamy white waterfall in the background, and beside you there's a huge bottle of Head & Shoulders shampoo. Or another girl, spinning in what looks like the ocean in huge waves which, though threatening, look as though they are caressing her skin – and which get smaller and smaller until they go into a Whirlpool washing machine. Another gorgeous woman is running in her white shoes on a rainy day, jumping over muddy puddles on narrower and narrower paths until coming to a halt on the edge of a deep canyon on a sunny day, and this is when the camera pans up to the sky and over the bottomless ravine, which is like the one Thelma and Louise sailed into in their car.

My mother wanted me to tell her about this sensation of being small and insignificant, wearing the latest brand of athletic shoe, in this immense earthly loneliness. People are not that familiar with Earth, with its water, its winds, its mud: they are just fooling themselves about being friends with Mother Nature, about geography being their second home. My mother was seeking the precise moment when publicity unveils the prank. Advertising prefers to transform the inhabitable into a familiar space, but my mother had not lost hope that one day those ads would end up telling the truth about the wilderness and its implacable laws.

My mother let herself be charmed by these false images of peaceful cohabitation between people and nature. A woman spreads happiness around her even on a filthy pathway. She is Youth and Beauty.

Look at this ad for a new make of car, a red one – they are all red – leaving behind deep tracks and clouds of dust across a burning desert without a single soul around. What is a single woman doing in the desert? How did she get there, and where is she going with such a deep cleavage, dressed in a see-through skirt? Before getting the message about the hybrid car, my mother could hardly believe anyone could imagine an almost naked woman crossing the desert alone. What about the deadly rays burning her skin? The sweat that makes you as salty as a hot dog? The scorpions?

And how about driving a black jeep across the Great White North? Wrapped up in a coat with a fur-lined hood, this woman gets out of the car in the middle of the immaculate vastness to sip coffee from her thermos bottle. The sun is shining over the horizon and the snow is gleaming like a mirror. In her way, she also seems familiar with this empire of eternal coldness and polar bears. My mother is jealous of her for being able to drink coffee at the North Pole, next to an Inuit fishing in a hole cut in the ice – and for being able to eat dinner that evening in a chic restaurant on St. Catherine Street, say, in Montreal.

This is why my mother wanted me to take this opportunity to spy on the moment when publicity sweeps away the boundaries imposed by human imagination. She was sending me to experience those short moments of advertising which elude the laws of reality and credibility. A woman, always young and beautiful, can cross the desert in a miniskirt and pat a polar bear. Advertisements annihilate the time before and the time after – everything that leads up to the moment and ends up a real story. Isn't it wonderful to live this everlasting present when a woman swims into the ocean of a washing machine?

Before I could make up my mind, Yannis's message came in response to mine.

Re: Lads
My lads? They are good guys. Only…

Reduced to an oppressively long wait, my comrades take on some bad habits that everyone can see, they can see it themselves. But who cares to improve in circumstances like these? They become lazy and impulsive and their life is reduced to increasingly disgusting habits: they scratch their dandruff and rub their testicles in sight of everyone. They admit they're weak, even if sometimes they're eager to act heroically, to endure some memorable ordeal to show them they can do better than hanging around ruined villages and pacing quiet streets.

Fear reveals itself in us as aggression and scorn. You can't imagine how other people's vices make community life unbearable. We get used to everybody's need to speak out, to tell stories, this human habit that puts you in contact not with people's real thoughts, but with their own fantasies about imaginary selves. The smallness of the common room where we live obliges us to listen to unbelievable boasts of prowess and dirty stories about women and sex. Other times we deal with hypochondriacs who do everything to convince us how sick they are and how intense is the pain they are feeling. Nobody takes this tissue of lies seriously, but we cannot stand not talking and listening. We listen idly, unable to contradict, to deny, or even to ask for a better version. This life brings out our worst faults.

The longer we stay here, the less we take care of

ourselves. Little by little, we stop bothering to shave and shower, as these habits are related to the desire to be liked, and who could like you in this desert? What you see every day are just gloomy faces, often dirty, for dust sticks to your skin like a mask. The energy that should shine out of a young face fades away. Nobody is interested in reading what is hidden behind this mask of wrinkles, hair, marks, and pimples. Inactivity annihilates the cooperation that should exist between body and spirit.

It is seldom that a mission that is more dangerous than usual can awaken courage, even heroism in us. The muggy atmosphere and the secrets of the uncertain day head cause everyone to let themselves go.

The most difficult thing is that we cannot isolate ourselves from the others. Life in a group can be oppressive. We hate the mass, while understanding we cannot survive without it. Loneliness is so dangerous here; a wounded animal taken away from the herd becomes vulnerable prey, easily hunted down by its natural enemies. The fact that in the army you don't choose your own friends or decide your own actions is reassuring, but it also drives you crazy. Next to your comrade you know you are safe, even when you despise him. The only way people can protect their intimacy against the invasion of others, is to build an imaginary space with transparent, sturdy walls.

Y

My mother knew I was in love, and she was suffering. One day she told me: wait for him to return. It was already too late for this shy warning. I loved the soldier for reasons that she did not fail to understand. Not my mother.

The height of any love story is always the sexual act, but maybe there is something even more gripping when this cannot take place. My mother knew I lacked both humour and a spirit of adventure. She also knew very well that nothing would persuade me to renounce this correspondence which dug deep into the heart of the blue-eyed soldier. And how did it happen that a Greek had blue eyes?

Yannis was not really handsome, but he looked strong. And every woman is sensitive to this characteristic, as we are all searching instinctively for a good father for our children.

In a picture he sent me, taken in front of the Canadian flag on the day he left for Afghanistan, he is looking somewhere above the head of the photographer. You can only see his left hand, lying on the bag hanging from his neck. What touched me was his black watch, a very cheap black watch around his wrist. This single detail made me feel so close to him, and I thought that the day we met I would give him a nice watch.

Are there any other secrets this picture could reveal about the man talking to me from these messages, telling me about a war that kept us apart? Would he like to come back home soon? Had his future projects changed in any way since he had got to know me? I did not know how to talk to him about everything on my mind. Instead, I asked him why everybody complained about the war in Afghanistan despite the enthusiastic beginnings.

Re: War

Any history book tells us that people learn more from defeat than from victory. The worst thing for us is that we do not know if we have won or if what we are living here is a discouraging defeat. Have we lost this war? I think this is the general perception that people have

of us and our mission, and it prevents them from seeing our small achievements here. We are trying hard
to convince villagers to stay close and remain loyal to
their government, dishonest as it is. Police fail in their
duty to provide security and confidence. People don't
trust anyone except the army, but the villagers we care
for today will be tomorrow's victims.

What drives us crazy is the public hypocrisy in our own
country, as at home even those who are generally op-
posed to war, or to this particular war, feel they have
to support the troops in Afghanistan. But how do you
support the troops and not the mission? What are we
supporting if not the need for them to die? So why are
there all those tears and accusations each time a soldier
is killed? In the collective sub-consciousness, a soldier's
mission in Afghanistan is to stay alive no matter what,
and the price is paid in other people's lives – the casualties among villagers nobody is even counting any more.

As long as the general attitude remains half-hearted,
and the government does not invest enough, we will
not be able to win this war. It is enough to see that in
any debate on this subject people try hard to avoid the
word war. From a personal and immediate conflict,
through to television, Afghanistan became a distant
problem disconnected from the real life of the West; it
is just a nasty place that produces caskets and pictures
of national funerals. But we are at war, damn it, and to
win the war they have to treat us as warriors, not social
workers. We are not the local police, busy directing
traffic and making the Taliban pay fines for drinking
and driving or for parking infractions. All we can do
is wait to return home, and try not to get killed in the
meantime. Which is not a whole lot for a fighter, right?

That day, I had to go to the head office of the advertising company for a photographic session. Behind the desk, a young woman and an old man examined me coldly. I was not really a star, as to get this status I should have achieved something more than smiling from a magazine cover. This meant I could not become the image of luxury goods like perfumes, cosmetics and cars. Those are fields reserved for real celebrities, who usually do more than pose for a ranking of the best universities.

The best things for people like me were food and detergents. I could play the role of an Italian cousin who brings over a new tomato sauce recipe to his overseas family; or I could be the upstairs neighbour complaining about stains on her white blouse or angrily rubbing soap scum off the shower stall. In her colourful apron, a stay-at-home mom always remains young and smiling. How could anyone trust products praised by a fat and wrinkled woman?

In the end, they decided the best I could do was to appear in a commercial about the new Campbell's Mushroom Soup. I would be the ideal mom of the ideal family living in the ideal house. My husband, a little fleshy but not overly so, his curls showing his few grey hairs, is sitting around the table next to our two children: a boy and a girl. The perfect dining room is next to the perfect kitchen, which is shining with neatness, as its appliances are never used except to heat up canned food and defrost frozen meals.

Hardly surprising, then, that you see no crumbs, no dirty towels, no forgotten mugs or spoons, not even a dishwasher full of dishes waiting for somebody to put them back in the cupboard. In this kitchen you always see more and more absorbent ScotTowels, spotless kitchen gloves (since no one uses them), and an empty sink with gleaming faucets. The counters are free of tableware except for a crystal vase with freshly cut flowers, and the refrigerator is full of food stored in plastic or paper containers, never in saucepans. On the stovetop, there is nothing cooking on the burner.

So this family of four happily looks at one another while sipping microwaved Campbell's soup. Through the big windows we see a lush garden on a wonderful summer day. The lawn is green, and flowers are in full bloom; after dinner the children rush outside to play in this earthly Eden. Behind them, the mother, wearing a well-ironed apron, and with not a hair out of place, smiles at the father, who gives her a look full of love.

I accepted this offer, even though I knew how my mother would react. You couldn't pull the wool over her eyes when it came to the way a kitchen looks. She knew too well the odours produced when you cook a really good soup. She knew what a counter looks like after you have chopped onions, carrots, celery, and tomatoes on it. She could talk a lot about the smell of boiling meat drifting into all the corners of the house, reaching even the neighbours' bedrooms. She could provide even more detail about the amount of dirty snow piling up under the window of our kitchen. And what about the ideal family? You would have to look hard to find such a pretty couple blessed with such nice, smiling children.

Once at home, I wrote Yannis a short message, without mentioning my publicity session. At the end of it, I asked him if he was scared of dying.

Re: Die

When you're alone, you think a lot about death, and this is dangerous. Fear transforms us into odious people, badly behaved. I think we should live in sweet ignorance of death. The good part, though, is that faced with danger, people ask themselves more often if they are happy.

Y

I took advantage of Yannis being around to ask him about the ordinary people he met over there. Despite the gap between the two sides, they were leading a modern war where people were in close touch, able to look into one another's eyes. What did the civilians think?

Re: Civilians

The civilians' philosophy of life boils down to this: Let them kill each other! Their indifference towards us seems very reasonable to me, as we carry out justice in this place without involving ourselves either in their society or in their religious cause. Simply put, we find those causes futile if not barbaric. Our approach is blind, and because of this, treachery, duplicity and lies rule everywhere, at every level. We are losing the final battle as we steer clear of what motivates their hatred and their actions.

To avoid danger, we just treat them all as spies, as Taliban disguised as civilians. On their side, they consider us nothing more than smiling, naive guys with a lot of energy. Their eyes, however, warn us never to forget to be afraid. We are exhausted by our own attempts to guess what is hidden behind the mask of their face. Their physiognomy is so treacherous: sometimes their sunburned faces emanate beauty and sweetness, but the next moment you are astonished by how they can reveal cruelty and ugliness. Their eyes stare at you with such intensity, ready to cut you into pieces, tear at your skin, scratch your cheeks. Their presence around us is over- whelming, hypnotic. The strangest thing is that they are cruel without selfishness. This disparity comes from the fact that we are so different from each other. Or it could be the fact that, armed as we are, from head to toe, we don't give them any chance to approach our body, to touch even a small piece of our flesh. Our eyes are hid- den behind sunglasses, and this gangster-like accessory warns them that contact with us is impossible, even as human contact here is as vital as the air we breathe.

At least we Canadians have a good reputation. We are different from the Europeans, they say. We believe eve- rything they tell us, and we pay the price they ask for any service, without bargaining. By this I understand we are the most naive of all the Westerners they know. Young Afghans are eager to do business with us, as we know how to lose without making a fuss. Our Ca- nadian identity is helpful and highly prized because they all know we are defending their country in other nations' interest, and for this reason they pity us. Even enemies who attack us in the dark kill us without hate. They trap us in an explosive blast just because we are strangers, as in this country, from the dawn of time, strangers have been abhorred and hunted down.

On our side, we also kill them by tradition and because the British army did it a long time ago. In a way, Cana- da continues the British invasion of their territories. A few of my guys have learned enough history to know how subjects of the British Crown broke their necks in a narrow mountain pass, 200 years ago. We could break our necks in these places, too, and Her Majesty the Queen would not care much.

In the afternoon, I got another message from Yannis:

Re: Taliban.

As we are talking about people, I know what your next question will be. I know you are dying to learn more about the Taliban's bravery, if these turbaned men are as cruel and savage as people in the West believe. I have a day off, so I will go ahead of your curiosity.

People tell the most incredible legends of the Afghan warriors' bravery, while for me their endurance is just a form of survival. They are as resistant as camels: able to fast an entire week so that they can then wolf down ten meals at once when they can afford it. What drives me crazy is not knowing much about the guy who is crawling along walls or blind fences. Who is Communist and who is Taliban among them? What regime did he serve? Or what faction of what regime? What characterizes this country is that within the same government there are as many rivals as tribes. We kid ourselves that we can reconcile them to one another, for what they hate most is the idea of living in peace with people in the next village or the nearby valley. Our efforts are just another big game that nobody takes seriously.

Communism, Capitalism, Islamism. Every doctrine loses its strength in these places, as every time people embrace new ideals it's only by necessity, not by conviction. Moderates are rare, as when these people embrace faith, they go to extremes. Among the villagers, there are veterans from all the conflicts that have devastated this place over the past quarter of a century.

There are people who believed and fought for Communism, then afterwards changed sides to fight with the mujahedeen chasing away the Soviets, alongside the Pakistanis. Later on, it was the Taliban's turn. When religious students from Pakistani madrassas arrived, people quickly joined their ranks, as the fundamentalists were able to deliver them from the cruel mujahedeen who were raping and killing women in the middle of the street within sight of everyone. Men let their beards grow and put black turbans on their heads. Nevertheless, the charm did not last long. The rapes stopped, but the new masters started whipping women whenever they saw the top of their shoes.

After the defeat of the Taliban, men shaved their beards and started learning English to do business with strangers. We are surrounded by friends and traitors. The worst thing is we can neither hate them nor chase them away, as they do nothing wrong. They act according to their nature and their customs. Tomorrow, my friend Rasul will betray me for sure. He will deliberately tell the Taliban the hour and the route taken by our convoy. And if I have a slight chance to escape alive, I cannot even be angry with him.

Finally, we are not here to crush the Taliban, and there are not any Taliban who would defeat us. It is this country that bests us, as no foreign government can rule it. We hold temporary control over their towns, while the rest of the territory remains under the authority of locals obeying ancestral laws that transcend any foreign domination. This hostile land is ungovernable. Within their different tribes nobody thinks it important to live and build together. Life is so difficult that mere survival is the greatest achievement. Nationality and identity have no great value. What matters is to eat and be warm.

The Taliban are a vivid incarnation of this country, which was never a colony, despite the fact that Europe was always present at its borders. Because of the spirit that governs people like these, who are all too normal here, strangers have always been depicted as stupid, from generation to generation, as they returned to their own countries with their tails between their legs. Today, we are the stupid ones, defeated by mountains, by cold, by the desert.

Y

At university, things were getting worse each day. My fame was the problem, especially since *Maclear's* had suggested I go to Afghanistan to encourage the Canadian troops. My classmates realized this story was getting serious, and I had to agree.

The news did make me realize how much I wanted to see Yannis. The distance that kept us far from each other and the time before he got to come home on leave had become unbearable. I wanted to see this man, look him in the eyes, and tell him about myself. Everything that happened so far seemed so fake: I was ashamed and I wished all this would stop once and for all. I was longing to talk about myself, as he was able to talk about himself at war. I had had enough of being a pin-up girl. I wanted to become a woman loved by a soldier. The fact that *Maclear's* took the initiative was maybe a good sign.

When I showed my mother the item in the magazine, her face changed on the spot. She said, "Tell Yannis about this. I think the magazine gets there almost at once."

I did what my mother suggested. His two days of silence were not due to a mission but because he was feeling bitter. My mother had figured that out. In a very short message he asked me if I wanted to become today's Marilyn Monroe, the sweetheart of the Canadian troops.

My mother wasn't surprised by his reaction. "He feels abandoned. You belong to him. He's jealous but he doesn't have the courage to accept it, as he thinks you will make fun of him. At war, men are much more possessive, as they are fighting for values prized by everybody in the world: peace and family. Have you ever heard of a soldier pinning up photographs of his wife for all his comrades to see?"

For the first time in my life, I regretted not having a woman friend. Talking to someone of your own kind becomes urgent in these moments of doubt. I wanted to listen to my own voice telling someone I love Yannis, that I want to touch him so much or just rub the collar of his shirt. For the first time, I could not share my thoughts with my mother, as what she always told me was just, "Wait for him to come back."

I replied to Yannis that the *Maclear's* story was not my idea, and I had no intention of parading in front of the Canadian army, dressed up in a miniskirt. I told him to forget this incident and instead, to tell me if he had any friends among the locals.

Re: Friends?

Yes, I have a friend, if I can call him that. The reason he is interested in me remains mysterious if not scary to me. I presume his curiosity about a foreign soldier hides intentions other than those he articulates. This small man, with evasive eyes, seems to me to be different from one day to the next. His attitude towards me is probably modified by secret events that happen in his village during the night, in the back of shadowy, unfurnished rooms. We are far from understanding what happens in his family or his neighborhood, what their fears are, and what they know about the Taliban, who continuously harass and threaten them.

Why do I still hesitate to call him a friend despite our daily conversations and the warmth he shows me? Because in a friendship the two people have to be equal. Wine is not the same as water or oil. And we are those different elements with different colours and densities which try to mix and make a drinkable beverage. What is unbearable to Rasul is that, in his opinion, I have no God. If I do not trust Allah, I should hurry to find out my own divinity, as quickly as possible – Buddha, Jesus, whoever. He is convinced that those small gods exist for real, but they are not his own.

Rasul is 22 years old. The day I met him for the first time, I told myself he looked a little bit like a fool, a cruel fool. His gestures were supple, like those of a panther, and his apparent stillness was a trick to hide the moment when he would attack me. In his placid eyes I could read what he was going to tell me one day about one of his friends, a mujahedeen veteran: "He washed his hands in the blood of our invader."

What disturbs Rasul most is my overseas life. He wants to know what else a human being could do, if he does not take care of animals, work in the fields, or feed a brood of kids. For him, what Westerners are good at is devoting their lives to manufacturing cars. Does this make them happy? Not necessarily, I assure him each time he asks me. And he agrees with this, as he believes people cannot be happy in big cities. The West is evil; he is convinced of this. I acknowledge that in the city where I live people tell very good lies. This confidence creates peace between us for a while.

What I appreciate most is his apparent modesty, even knowing that this attitude is entirely fake. I am simply not used to a man openly manifesting his ignorance, his shame of not knowing things, and his desire to improve himself. Unfortunately, language is a big barrier between us, as the few words he has learned from Canadian soldiers are not enough to allow him to express his ideas properly or ask questions. In his attitude I see how he has made peace with his life as it is, so hopeless and lacking in comfort. His face, still young, loses its human brilliance to acquire instead the pallor of an inanimate object. Sometimes, under the cruel light of the sun, his cheeks look like snake-skin, while at other times they are more like dry tree bark.

I have to go now.

Y

I was grateful that he was saying no more about *Maclear's* blunder. I knew, though, that Yannis was terribly hurt, and that jealousy bit into his soul. Despite my denial, I think he still believed I was the one who had initiated this idea. And he was right to doubt my sincerity, as even my mother looked at me suspiciously.

Would I have agreed to march in front of Canadian soldiers who had only had pictures of naked women to look for months past? He surely knew that every woman's mind is dominated by the desire to see a herd of males around her, fighting for her charms. In nature, females always choose among those who battle one another for the right to get them pregnant. Why have people reduced a woman's chance of selecting the most handsome man? Yannis was right to mistrust me.

What about him though? Did he not have any secret admirers around? I did not wait for him to continue his account about his friend Rasul. I asked him instead to tell me stories about Afghan women.

Re: Women

In our garrison people often talk about cases involving women mutilated by their husbands. Why do you think this kind of story occupies a soldier's mind more than others? Because in this kind of tragedy, repeated for the benefit of every new recruit, there is a secret desire for them to save the Beauty and to deliver her from the Beast. Their imagination makes up this soap opera in which they play the charming prince, buckled under the weight of their ammunition. They dream of taking these desperate beauties out of the hands of their bearded and primitive aggressors.

In their stories, though, the lascivious women's bodies are hardly dressed, or they wear some Scheherazade-like transparent veil. They voluntarily forget the precarious life they lead, the worn burkas and dusty dresses they put on every day, as what this country most lacks is water. I have read that the Afghan people are very clean and that they like washing several times a day, but I wonder how and when, as water is as rare as gold, and it is difficult to get it even to cook.

You can guess that I am not innocent either of this

fantasizing. The desert and the mountains feed these sick imaginings, as our minds try to annihilate a frightening reality.

In spite of all, I think we are here for Afghan women. As for concrete stories, believe me I know nobody personally. I can only reproduce what my friend Rasul tells me on this matter. And for sure he tells me some exaggerated versions to amuse me, to exchange information with me, and to practice his English. However, what is normal for Rasul is dark and unbearable to me. What I understand from my friend is that there is really no comparison between our two worlds. This is why sometimes I feel we are here just for these women. From all I see around me, it is their life that seems the most horrible. What they undergo every day makes me violent and ready to provide a weak justification for each new murder my lads commit.

The harsh reality is that we came from afar just to watch them through sunglasses, as we can do nothing. And the truth is that women must liberate themselves before they can free themselves from the tyranny of man.

I'm going to tell you Hamid's story, one of my other local acquaintances. He is a driver for some foreigners here. This does not prevent him from doing all kinds of other jobs in order to make ends meet. He often comes to offer me Afghan jewellery weighing more than a kilo, as it's made of raw lapis lazuli. He lives alone as his wife is in jail. He married her when she was 14, but after a year she was imprisoned for adultery. He does not want to provide any other details, except the few English words he knows best: "Women, bad, very bad."

Rasul however knows more of this story, and he tells me the truth is quite different. He says that Hamid's family, his father and two other brothers, have lived off their women's prostitution. This started a long time ago, under the Soviet period, when his mother was raped by a mujahedeen commander during a raid against the Red army. This tragic event, however, prompted the father to get into the sex trade before he was killed by another mujahedeen. The boys had to carry on this business in order to survive the famine.

When Hamid got married, he asked his wife to replace his mother, who was now too old to attract men. Instead of obeying him, she called the police and denounced him. The Taliban, who were by now in control, arrested Hamid and imprisoned him, but they later freed him. Things were much worse for his little wife. Publicly whipped and stoned for having stood up to her family, she too was thrown into jail. After the Taliban's defeat and departure, prisoners were released, but no one knew what had become of Hamid's wife.

I think he would very much like to find his wife, but only to punish her in his own way. Prisons are never a solution for women, and everybody avoids putting them in jail, as this serves nobody. Women are punished here for what seems to be the worst sin, zina, which implies sex in all possible versions. Be it broken marriages, violence, prostitution – everything comes under the umbrella of zina, for which any woman can be repudiated or killed without due process.

When it comes to sex, women are never in the right when they're up against men. And if a woman has sinned, why put her in jail, where nobody can reach and punish her as she deserves? An ordeal does not have to be individual but is sometimes collective, as this is the only way of reestablishing the social order. A woman who is not within a man's reach does not really pay for her mistakes.

Despite what she has suffered, Hamid considers his wife remains unpunished. Her own version of the facts does not matter at all, and everybody agrees she should have stayed in the village regardless. Hamid cannot bear to feel humiliated, which is why he always tells the story of adultery, which absolves him and saves him from providing some of the other details.

Hamid does not seem a bad man and, though everybody knows his story, nobody hates him. In fact, what right do you have hating or despising anyone here? People barricade themselves behind the fact that these are local customs, and no one goes any farther. My buddy Simon is the only one who dares ask Hamid for details, but this curiosity about sordid things angers Hamid. Despite his interest in maintaining good relationships with us, he shouts at Simon, "Dirty, Dirty." They do things, but at least they do not talk about them. They hide their shame, if any, under silence. They try to heal themselves by keeping quiet.

In our garrison we don't have much to say about women whose life is made hell by other women within their own family, such as sisters, aunts, mothers-in-law and even mothers. The harm women inflict on each other is unthinkable. What shocked me was the story Rasul told me one day about one of his sisters-in-law, aged 16, who had just given birth. In fact, he wanted to impress me with his relative's heroism, especially as she had delivered a boy: if she had had a girl, her suffering would not have warranted the same admiration. The fact that his brother was now father to a boy was reassuring. Rasul hoped this would help end his arguments with his wife.

He told me admiringly about this young woman's pain. For me this was in fact an unappealing picture of hospitals, of the doctors and nurses working there, because sometimes they offer no assistance to women who struggle alone like animals, under other future mothers' eyes, waiting their turn to give birth.

When a woman is considered bad, like Hamid's wife, there is even less compassion: and often young brides only ten years old die during miscarriages with no one at their side. Few women pity their unfortunate sisters who are beaten and obliged to immolate themselves to escape violence. They too believe that only bad women have a bad destiny.

Fathers are not to blame when they pay their family's debts by selling their daughters or when they marry them off to men twice their age or to men who are already married. Once the dice are thrown and a woman's destiny is settled, what happens next – plotting, violence, suicide – is all her own fault. Older women share the same conviction as their husbands that young girls are sexually insatiable, tempting men and inciting them to sin. They too would tell you that that is the rule in their country and everybody should respect it. No wonder the government uses foreign aid to build more prisons, bigger than the older ones. If there is any progress here it is that nowadays women are put into jail instead of delivering them to tribal mercy. Rasul told me his own cousin Latifa's story. He asked me if in my country women have to bleed during their first night with their husband. Bluntly put, is it mandatory for a bride to be a virgin? He already knew the answer, but he wanted to show me, comparatively, how morals are purer here. How could a man be content with somebody else's leftovers? Obviously, a woman's hymen is a warrant for moral purity.

So, his cousin Latifa was married at 12 years of age. The auspices were good as her future husband was quite young, not yet married, neither ugly nor too violent. Nevertheless, Latifa had the bad luck not to bleed during her deflowering. As it happens, one of the doctors temporarily working in the village tried to convince the two men in the family that this act sometimes happens without causing bleeding. He even explained to them that there were seven types of vagina and in two cases out of seven women do not bleed during their first sexual act. Rasul was astonished by this doctor trying to trick the father and the groom. Obviously the two men were not that stupid as to believe this nonsense about seven vaginas. Lately, people had had enough bad experiences with doctors educated abroad, encouraged by foreigners to encroach upon their traditions.

After weeks of torture while the husband tried to make Latifa confess her sin, he finally threw her out. The poor girl first knocked on her father's door, but her own brother savagely beat her and left her in the middle of the street. It was the only way for them to wash her of sin and save the family's honour. After that, they lost track of her. Nobody gave a damn; it was as though she were dead.

Later, they found out she had been caught by two policemen, who had spotted her in the street as she was walking unaccompanied by a male family member. They took her into their office and raped her many times in other men's company, after which they did her the favour of not putting her in jail but left her in the street again. Everybody has lost count of how many times she was raped as a woman alone in the street.

When she was finally brought into hospital on a stretcher, Latifa asked a nurse what she should do. The nurse answered that suicide was the best solution. She even advised her on a way to do it: immolation. This is what Latifa tried to do, but unsuccessfully. Clumsily, she only sprayed her feet with gas, hoping that the flames would set fire to the rest of her body. But while her feet were burning she was not able to endure the pain anymore and started rolling around on the ground. She was saved with her legs burned right to the bones.

Where was she now and what was her future? What happened to her was preferable, said Rasul, as other women who abandoned their family were living as prostitutes, and even drinking, smoking and taking drugs. Latifa was a nightmare for her family. Rasul cited to me the Afghan saying about the three big dangers that threaten their social order: *zan, zar, zamin* – woman, gold, land. Even though veiled and without freedom, women were the worst of all evils. Lafita's case was the best example.

In all this, and despite the tyranny exerted by men upon women, there is nevertheless a divine revenge, as even Rasul has to run away from home to escape arguments between his sisters, wives, sisters-in-law and mothers-in-law. They quarrel all day long over small things, be it the best place near the fire, a piece of soap, or a dirty rug. The women of the family are pitiless with one another. It is easy to imagine that they apply to their sisters the same ill-treatment that men inflict upon them. A woman is the only individual with whom another woman can argue in the house.

I have to go. If everything goes well, I will be back tomorrow morning.

Y

To my letter, "Are you back?," Yannis answered two days later.

Re: Are you back?

The power shut down because of a small shooting. No casualties though.

Marching in front of the garrison, I met Azuz, Rasul's friend. He too seeks out my company, but he is very different from Rasul, even if he wears the same clothes and his features speak of the same tribal origin. He is also a Pashtun, but God knows from which branch of the tribe. Each new day, Rasul tells me another story about his friend, and I imagine this is because of his poor English. Maybe it is just the fact that he only knows a few words that makes him forget what he said the day before. Each time we talk about Azuz, he adds strange new events to his biography, worried only about pronunciation and awkward new words, without paying attention to the different meanings he evokes. Yesterday, for example, he told me that Azuz was educated in a Pakistani madrassa, and that this explains his friend's admiration for our group of men. The orphans born and raised in Pakistan are almost exclusively educated in refugee military camps, without any contact with women. Young men who come from that indoctrinated milieu have neither family nor roots. Little boys are fed all their lives by foreign aid, they are deprived of any lay education, they ignore the traditional arts and crafts, and they do not experience the affective bonds that link members in a tribal society. Their interests are exclusively related to war and blood. This may explain why Azuz is so grim about the fact that there is nothing wrong with the punishment inflicted on disobedient women: they should remain inside the house forever. From his childhood he has been taught that women are just bad seeds, temptations that lead men astray.

In the light of these revelations I understand why Azuz is so attracted by a manly way of life, like ours. Foreign troops look like old religious orders to him. In a way, he really admires us, the invaders. Azuz looks at me passionately each time I touch my clothes, rub my ears, or loosen the strap on my helmet. My body is like a show he does not want to miss. We, too, are living a manly life, a military brotherhood, away from any womanly touch or presence. They keep women away by education and we, by fear. Those veiled women awake in us no desire, as we are not used to guessing the beauty hidden underneath their thick dresses. Azuz's erotic fantasies are stimulated by even a delicate movement of a dark veil.

Despite his many faults, Rasul seems to me a man educated by tradition. He knows by heart the genealogy of his tribe and of his own family, and he is very proud of it. He knows many legends that he is not able to recount in detail, but his gestures are clear enough for me to get their essence. The traditional anti-feminist culture nonetheless leaves him with a certain tolerance mixed with a lot of envy of the weaker sex. Under the pleats of their dresses and veils, women are not just shadows or evil ghosts but humans endowed with a soul. Rasul has two daughters whom he does not seem to discriminate against compared with his sons. Sometimes he comes to see me accompanied by one of them, the one who is always sick and snotty, wrapped up in thread-bare sweaters and wearing her mother's ragged slippers. Rasul knows that the soldiers will give her candies and chewing gum and even some Kleenex. However, she always uses her sleeves to clean up her abundant snot as her mother uses the Kleenex to light the fire. I have to leave. I will be back in the evening, a little later though.

Y

You will have seen on TV that Corporal Yannis Alexandridis died in a bomb blast while he and two other soldiers were on a mission to provide food to a garrison in a nearby village.

I, too, heard the news on TV. Nobody mentioned our relationship, and I did not go to his funeral, which was in Montreal. I did not want to meet his mother and his sister, each of them what the Archbishop had called a Lilly crying over the death of the man in their family.

I did not give Yannis the opportunity to know I loved him. I was ashamed to acknowledge how much I needed him and that it isn't only countries that have to be defended but individuals, too. If I did, he would not have died. My love would maybe have played a role, choosing him for life and not for death.

I refused him moments that should have been ours alone; I did not guess our relationship would be so short. I would have been very happy if he had treated me as his wife just for three weeks. Unfortunately, it's war that cancels out the possibility of becoming, or simply of continuing to be what you are.

The next day, everyone forgot the incident. North America does not give people much time for regret. Someone who mourns too long ends up on the psychiatrist's couch. People believe in a quick healing. Love, death, failure – nothing lasts long.

I forgot to tell you about Maisonneuve's death. That was the best part of the religious plays we made up in Marika's basement. My friend understood all too well what must have been in this man's heart when he returned in France, defeated and humiliated.

After being banished from his post, Maisonneuve did not go back to the mansion inherited from his father. He preferred to settle in Paris, a crowded city, where he rented a room for himself and his servant Louis Fin. After a while, he decided to travel a little through Europe. First, he went to Brittany, and then he headed to Amsterdam to see paintings by a painter called Rembrandt. In one of his tableaux, the painter depicted Paul from the shadows, wearing a ridiculous bonnet, with his cheeks hollow and his eyes teary. This is what Maisonneuve had become.

He did not stay abroad any longer. He went back to Paris to dwell in the house of the Fathers of Christian Doctrine, on Fossés-Saint-Victor. In the small garden behind the house, he built a Canadian-style wooden cabin for Canadian visitors coming to Paris. Despite his timidity and his secluded life, he was easy to spot. His strong carriage, his height and his dark skin, tanned from long exposure to the sun, were difficult to overlook in a Parisian crowd. Traders regularly saw him along the narrow streets, hobbling from the pain in his left leg.

The faithful Louis Fin, who had followed him into exile, shared his retirement. His life as a servant was quiet, as his master had very modest tastes. Maisonneuve was never a demanding man, and at this time he was even steadier than before and easy to satisfy. His only excess was the time he asked for a flautist to come and play for him. Like Jeanne Mance on the shores of the St. Lawrence, he was quietly preparing for death.

What occasionally disturbed his daily routine was the arrival of a deputation from Montreal looking for money from rich benefactors. That was the only thing that awoke him from his torpor, and he did everything in his power to help them. To celebrate their presence, he himself went to the nearby shop to buy a bottle of good wine. He even unlocked his wooden case to retrieve those old documents that had declared him Governor of Montreal. After their departure, he withdrew into his loneliness again.

As the difficult emotions experienced in Ville Marie faded away, he enjoyed a peaceful new life. From an active faith, he got used to detachment, patience, and silence. He died in a bed covered in furs, just as though he were lying in a Canadian cabin. He bequeathed all his belongings to the Notre Dame congregation and Hôtel Dieu of Montreal.

One day, Marika proposed that we change the story and make it so that Maisonneuve ended his days in Montreal with Jeanne. The brave soldier should never have returned to France. He should have died in his beloved Ville

Marie. The two old friends should have grown old together, even though they would have been appalled by the way people were now behaving in the colony. They would have been helpless witnesses to changes that flew in the face of all the pure convictions they had started out with. Their friendship, such a rare friendship, would have helped them to overcome their sorrows more readily.

After a few troubled years, the Montreal community began a new period of peace and prosperity under the authority of the new Governor, Jean Talon. Both Paul and Jeanne would have ended their days watching ships sailing downriver to Quebec, loaded with wood and pelts, while canoes paddled by Indians travelled back and forth between the north and south shores of the St. Lawrence.

Every Sunday, they would have walked side by side in the market at Place d'Armes, where they would have seen barrels of fish, furs stretched out in the sun so the pelts became glossy, and game hanging from iron hooks. The Indians, those formidable hunters who were the children Jeanne and Paul had once baptized, were carrying on the same trade as their parents before them, except that they were now exchanging furs for guns and alcohol.

Free now of their duties, it was only now that the two old friends could think about what their lives had been and what they might have become. They could even confess their passion, as Jeanne and Paul were undoubtedly in love with each other. What had prevented them from admitting their feelings were the daily uncertainties, the danger, and especially the example of morality they had to show their companions.

Jeanne and Paul had missed out on the opportunity to declare their love for each other when they were young. If now, in old age, they did finally admit their passion, they could end up reliving their missed youth. They would have talked about their vanished vigour and beauty, as neither Paul nor Jeanne was bad-looking. They would have amused themselves remembering the dresses Jeanne wore, so shabby and faded that nobody could tell what fabric they were made of. And what about that winter when Paul took down his own curtains to give to the tailor, Guillaume Chartier! And how many other things could they have told each other, as peace was restored within the colony. What religious fervour could prevent a man from falling in love with a woman?

My last thought is for my mother, who lives her own life in this mystic city, which was founded on behalf of a civilization of love, but who is still nostalgic about Greek muses. Is it true that when people get old they rejuvenate themselves with Greek civilization? Somebody said that this happens, particularly in dreams. For my mother this would be nice. Nothing can shock her, least of all the future.

The accelerating rhythms of newness make some people dizzy, but not my mother. She can no longer be astonished by the random piling on of events that turn our lives upside down. Her firm conviction is that the effects of war and migration on the human species are ways the past imposes itself on the present. She mourns losses like that Jewish woman, once upon a time, for each mother knows what hurts her offspring. This war had mortally wounded me, and there was nothing she could do.

If I were to give an account of my present life, I would see how unheroic it is. How many insignificant gestures a woman makes in order to survive in this mysterious sea of life. And how fateful are the consequences of every move she makes to keep the vessel of her existence afloat. I know what you think: I am too young to say that the best part of my life is behind me. But too many hurts suffered at an early age diminish one. I distrust pleasures still to come.

There are still people who ask me for interviews, even though everyone I know questions the role played by foreign troops in Afghanistan. Some of them think I'm someone who should support the war. I still accept their invitations to talk. Even if there is nothing to talk about, I hope my words will at least help preserve people's memories of the war.

As for me, since Yannis's death there is no afterwards. What I still have is this routine, with my mother. There is little chance of that being interrupted by anything else, for the postman never rings twice, if you know what I mean.

Acknowledgements

Although this novel was inspired by a true story, all the characters in the book are fictional. My first praise goes to *Maclean's* magazine for covering the astonishing story of a young woman and a Canadian soldier in the summer of 2007.

Despite the liberties I have taken in creating this work of fiction, there are writers who played a significant role in helping me – as I have never set foot in Afghanistan – to recreate the Afghan side of the story. I am happy to acknowledge my debt to the American journalist Ann Jones, whom I admire for involvement in the plight of Afghan women, which led her to write *Kabul in Winter* (Metropolitan, 2006); the Pakistani journalist Ahmed Rashid's *L'ombre des Taliban* (Autrement, 2001), which is essential reading for those interested in the nature of the conflicts in that part of the world; and Angelo Rasanayagam's *Afghanistan: A Modern History* (I. B. Tauris, 2003), an erudite journey into the history of this people.

In reconstructing the founding of Montreal, I spent many wonderful hours at the archives of the Bibliothèque et Archives nationales du Québec. It would be impossible to mention all the documents and maps I consulted, but I will single out *The People of New France* (University of Toronto Press, 1997) by Allan Greer, and *Jeanne Mance* (Bibliothèque québécoise, 2009), by Françoise Deroy-Pineau.

Of great help in finishing my novel was a grant from Conseil des arts et des lettres du Québec along with a residency at The Canadian Institute. The person who encouraged me to submit an application was Émile Martel from

PEN Québec, whom I thank once again.

My gratitude to Liz Brooks (now Robertson) for her English lessons, and to Sorel Freedman whose course on Canadian civilization at the Université de Montréal persuaded me to subscribe to *Maclean's*. Adela and Bogdan helped by making fun of my accent and the way I pronounce the words "idea" and "better," which sound to them like "ID" and "Beta." Calinic persuaded me not to listen to the children. Last but not least, I thank Linda, who made all this possible.